A HUSBAND'S KISS

"Do you know that you always smell of lilacs?"

"It is from the soap I use."

"Mmm . . . I like it," he whispered, moving to lightly nip the lobe of her ear. At the same moment his hands lifted to begin removing the pins from her hair in an impatient fashion.

Wondering how she could feel as if she were drowning when she was standing in the center of the library, Addy clutched at the lapels of his coat. Something seemed to be stirring deep within her. Something that was a mixture of pleasure, excitement, and a building need.

She closed her eyes as his seeking lips moved from her ear to the tender arch of her neck.

"What are you doing?" she demanded in a choked voice.

"I wish to see your hair about your shoulders." His fingers plunged into the heavy curls now freed from their tidy bun. "Such beautiful hair. Gypsy hair."

"Adam, I am not sure . . ."

"Just one kiss, Addy," he pleaded in husky tones. "One kiss that has nothing to do with duty or wifely obligation. One kiss that you give freely."

She should say no.

But even as the voice of caution whispered in the back of her mind, her lips were parting in silent invitation . . .

Books by Debbie Raleigh

LORD CARLTON'S COURTSHIP

LORD MUMFORD'S MINX

A BRIDE FOR LORD CHALLMOND

A BRIDE FOR LORD WICKTON

A BRIDE FOR LORD BRASLEIGH

THE CHRISTMAS WISH

THE VALENTINE WISH

THE WEDDING WISH

A PROPER MARRIAGE

Published by Zebra Books

A PROPER MARRIAGE

Debbie Raleigh

ZEBRA BOOKS
KENSINGTON PUBLISHING CORP.
http://www.kensingtonbooks.com

ZEBRA BOOKS are published by

Kensington Publishing Corp.
850 Third Avenue
New York, NY 10022

All Kensington titles, imprints and distributed lines are available at special quantity discounts for bulk purchases for sales promotion, premiums, fund-raising, educational or institutional use.

Special book excerpts or customized printings can also be created to fit specific needs. For details, write or phone the office of the Kensington Special Sales Manager: Kensington Publishing Corp., 850 Third Avenue, New York, NY 10022. Attn. Special Sales Department. Phone: 1-800-221-2647.

Zebra and the Z logo Reg. U.S. Pat. & TM Off.

First Printing: October 2002
10 9 8 7 6 5 4 3 2 1

Printed in the United States of America

To David,
For allowing me the gift of time

Prologue

As a rule Vicar Humbly did not believe in premonitions.

He was a sensible man who did not seek ominous omens or hope for miraculous messages from above. Such flamboyant symbols did not suit a simple vicar.

But this morning he could not deny a vague sense of unease.

Three letters.

All delivered in this morning's post.

Three letters from three separate brides, all of whom had haunted his conscience for the past several months.

Could it be a sign?

With a frown he tapped a finger upon his cluttered desk.

On first glance there was nothing in any of the letters to stir his concern. They contained nothing more than mundane details of the young ladies' days, local gossip, and a hope that he was doing well.

But the mere fact that he had often worried over the fates of Addy, Beatrice, and Victoria made him sensitive to the realization that none of them revealed the giddy happiness that surely should be apparent in the letters from a new bride.

Indeed, they were oddly stilted as if each were afraid of revealing too much in their guarded words.

His notoriously soft heart clenched at the thought that they were in any way unhappy.

Perhaps he should not have ignored the doubts that had plagued him before he had agreed to perform the weddings. Although the marriages had been months apart, he could not deny that each had made him hesitate. Deep inside there had been a decided fear that all was not well with the three couples.

Poor Addy Morrow being wed to Mr. Drake who deeply disapproved of her vivid spirit.

Beatrice Chaswell who Humbly feared was being wed for her large fortune.

And Victoria Mallory who had been unexpectedly compromised and forced into marriage with a complete stranger.

Three marriages that had been chosen for reasons other than love.

Hoping to clear his muddled thoughts, Humbly left his desk and slipped through the open door to the garden beyond.

There were few things more delightful than Surrey in April, he decided as he carefully bent down to weed around his beloved roses.

Rare sunlight dappled the countryside, warming the soft breeze that was liberally laced with the scent of wild flowers. Butterflies danced in twirling patterns, while newborn foals awkwardly stretched their legs in a nearby pasture.

Even the distinctly shabby Vicarage with its worn red bricks and slate roof acquired a mellow beauty in the golden glow.

It was a day to appreciate one's blessings, Humbly tried to tell himself. And he had a great deal to appreciate. A rich, full life in service of God. Remarkable health for a gentleman staring sixty directly in the eye. And dear friends that often filled the Vicarage.

And, of course, he would soon be leaving his duties to retire to a lovely cottage only a few miles away. At long last he would have ample time to devote to his garden and the freedom to indulge his fancy for titillating novels that he had always adored, but that had never seemed quite proper for a Vicar to read.

Yes, he should be in a joyous mood, he acknowledged with a faint sigh. But instead he found his thoughts dwelling upon those disturbing letters.

Could he truly retire in peace with the knowledge that three of the marriages he had blessed were in trouble?

Did he not have a duty to assure himself that he had done all that was possible to help those in his care?

He heaved yet another sigh as a shadow fell over him. Glancing up, Humbly regarded the iron gray hair and forbidding expression of the stout woman who towered over him.

Mrs. Stalwart had been the housekeeper at the Vicarage for the past thirty years. Like a seasoned general she kept his household running with a smooth perfection, turned aside those who would take advantage of his soft heart, and ensured that he was kept somewhat in order.

Not a day passed that he did not send up a small prayer of thanks for God's good sense in bringing Mrs. Stalwart to his life. Even if she did tend to scold him as if he were six rather than sixty.

As if to prove his point, the housekeeper placed her hands upon her ample hips and glared down at his rumpled form.

"I thought I would find you here."

"Oh, Mrs. Stalwart." He conjured his most innocent smile. "Is it time for tea?"

She gave a loud snort. "Tea will be served at four as

usual. I thought you were devoting the afternoon to sorting through the books in the library?"

"Yes, well, it was such a lovely day I decided to spend a few moments tending to the roses."

"Fah." The wily old woman was not fooled for a moment. "You are dawdling. Shall I attend to the books myself?"

Humbly shuddered in horror. Mrs. Stalwart might be the very best of housekeepers, but she had no love for his precious books. Given the opportunity she would no doubt pitch the lot of them in the nearest fire.

"Certainly not," he said firmly. "Only I know which references must remain and which I may take to the cottage."

Not about to be diverted, she lifted an iron gray brow. "Then make a list. I can read."

Ignoring the protest of his knees, Humbly rose to his feet. It was difficult to possess a measure of dignity while a large woman hovered over him.

"I am not leaving today, Mrs. Stalwart. It will be six months before the new Vicar arrives."

"Good thing, since you have not so much as packed a candlestick."

Too accustomed to the woman's gruff manner to take offense, Humbly merely smiled.

"Everything in its time, my good lady. We must enjoy what the Lord has given us this day. Beautiful sunshine, a lovely breeze. It would be a sin to waste such a blessing."

"You may save such sermons for the pulpit," she warned him, her shrewd gaze noting his air of distraction. "I know you far too well. Whenever you begin weeding the roses it is a sure sign that something is troubling you."

A faint hint of color touched his plump cheeks. It was disconcerting to realize he was so very predictable.

"Ah well, as one becomes old we must expect the occasional troubles. Aches and pains, and of course, one's digestion is always so unpredictable. I do hope Mrs. Graves has prepared a few of her lemon tarts for tea. They always settle my stomach.''

Distracted at last, Mrs. Stalwart lowered a disapproving gaze to his comfortably rounded midsection.

''You mean they settle around your stomach,'' she corrected. ''I have had to move the buttons on your waistcoat on three occasions during the past year. You will have to settle for cucumber sandwiches.''

Humbly grimaced in distaste. ''Judas.''

Unrepentant, the woman tapped an impatient foot upon the graveled path.

''And I was not speaking of your constitution. You have been fretting and brooding since the morning post arrived. Are you disappointed that a new Vicar has been chosen?''

''Gracious, no. I shall be quite happy to settle in my cottage with nothing to concern me beyond my garden,'' he was able to deny in all truth.

''Then what has you so unsettled?''

Realizing that the tenacious woman was not to be easily distracted, Humbly gave in to the inevitable.

'' 'From the fruit of his words a man is satisfied with good and the work of a man's hand comes back to him,' '' he quoted softly.

She offered him a puzzled frown. ''What does that mean?''

He gave a faint shrug. ''Perhaps it is only the eccentricities of an old man, but I can not leave my position with a clear conscience. Not when I fear that I have been neglectful in my duties.''

Mrs. Stalwart swiftly bristled with indignation at the hint he had somehow been remiss in his responsibilities.

''Absurd. You have dedicated yourself to your duties for forty years. How many nights have you gone out to comfort the sick and dying? Or trudged through the rain to visit the

orphanage? I should like to give anyone a piece of my mind
who would say you ain't done your duty.''

Humbly could not help but smile at the woman's fierce
loyalty. He did not doubt she would readily thrash anyone
daring to insult him within her hearing.

''Thank you, Mrs. Stalwart, but it is in my own heart that
I am uneasy.''

''What is it then?''

''Just an old man's fancy, no doubt, but I should like to
be sure,'' he murmured, his thoughts returning to the three
letters lying in his library. Dare he meddle in what was by
rights a holy sacrament between a man and a woman? Could
a feeble Vicar do more than cause even more troubles? Then
again, could he be satisfied if he did not make some sort of
effort? Dear heavens, it was all very confusing. Still, he
supposed that deep inside he had already made his decision.
If one of his flock was in need of him, then he could not
turn his back. ''God's will can occasionally use a helping
hand.''

''Does this mean you will not be packing away those
musty books?''

''Do not fret. I shall attend to them the moment I return.''

''Return? Where are you going?''

Humbly took a moment to consider. He supposed that it
was only sensible to impose some order on his vague plans.
Addy and Adam had been married the longest. He would
begin with them.

''I shall be traveling to London,'' he said in decisive
tones.

''London?'' Mrs. Stalwart was understandably shocked.
Humbly rarely traveled more than a few miles from the
Vicarage. He firmly believed his place was among his peo-
ple, not gadding about the more fashionable neighborhoods.
She gave a click of her tongue. ''I fear that the sun has gone

to your head. Return to the library and I will see to your tea.''

Not wishing to endure a lengthy lecture on the dangers of London, Humbly merely smiled with pleasure.

''Please do not forget the lemon tarts.''

''Cucumber sandwiches,'' she corrected, turning about her considerable bulk to march back into the Vicarage.

Sifting through the numerous details that would have to be attended to before he could comfortably travel to London, Humbly reached into his pocket and removed a napkin containing a lemon tart he had earlier filched from the kitchen.

At least in London he would be free to indulge his love for sweets, he thought with a faint smile.

He could only pray he was making the proper decision. And that he was not about to do more harm than good.

He had precious little experience in playing Cupid.

Chapter One

It was generally conceded that Adam Stonewell Drake was a gentleman of great presence.

Standing nearly six feet, he possessed a thick mane of dark hair that was liberally winged with silver and unnerving gray eyes that could make the most brazen soul tremble with unease. His features were lean, almost austere in their beauty. And his large form had been chiseled to hard, uncompromising lines.

But it was not just his noble bearing or physical perfection that created an image of formidable power. He was also an intelligent, well-spoken gentleman who demanded precise order in his life. Heaven help anyone foolish enough to interfere in his rigid schedule.

Adam paid little heed to his ominous reputation.

It was true that he preferred a well-regulated household and maintained a detailed schedule of his daily activities. And certainly he possessed little patience with those fribbles who preferred to waste their days upon fashion and gossip.

Such self-indulgence seemed to indicate a weak character. But he did not consider himself rigid or unyielding.

Or at least he had not until the past few weeks, he grimly acknowledged.

Pushing aside the schedule he had just completed, Adam sat back in his chair and laid his hands upon the polished desk.

He was seated in his library as he was every morning. There was a solid sense of security in the book-lined walls and mahogany furnishings. And of course, it was here that he maintained his vast collection concerning military history that had been his passion since his days at Oxford. It was a passion that had led to his current position at the War Department, offering his expertise in war strategies.

This morning, however, his gaze did not fondly linger upon the rare leather-bound books or large maps of the Continent that were tidily rolled up on a polished table. Instead he brooded upon the icy tension that filled the London townhouse.

He had expected his life to alter somewhat when he married Adele Morrow. It was inevitable that both would be expected to make compromises and adjust to living within the same household. But while he had prepared himself to endure occasional disruptions and even the inevitable confrontation, he was caught off guard by the disturbing chill that had grown steadily more pronounced between himself and his bride.

Damnation, he silently cursed, a slender finger tapping a frustrated tattoo upon his desk.

It was growingly obvious that his expertise in war strategies had been of precious little help when plotting a strategy for marriage.

He had been so certain that it was imperative that he instruct Addy upon what he expected from his wife. Surely it was best to have the ground rules out in the open, he had smugly decided.

And so, he had lectured her upon the proper conduct of a young lady, going so far as to make a meticulous list of behaviors that would and would not be suitable. And he had even personally chosen her wardrobe to ensure the gowns would be suitable.

After all, she had been born into a notoriously scandalous family. Lord Morrow was a lecher and a drunkard who readily made a fool of himself among society. Lady Morrow was hardly better with her eccentric habit of painting nude young men in her own drawing room. Even her elder brother had managed to cause gossip when he had set up household with a married countess and her five children.

How could he not be concerned by the distasteful influence her upbringing must have had upon Addy?

Especially when their marriage was not based upon mutual affection, but instead had been arranged years before by their respective grandfathers?

Addy was a tempestuous beauty with an impulsive nature, which he had often rued. It would be all too easy for her to blunder into scandal without realizing the danger to their position in society. It only made sense to avert disaster before it was too late.

All very reasonable. Unfortunately he had miscalculated the effects of his well-intended efforts.

Addy had indeed become the very model of propriety. Her bold, dashing manner was now thoroughly subdued. She dressed modestly, her raven curls were painfully scraped into a knot and she rarely left the townhouse.

Precisely what he requested, but Adam could not deny that beneath the cool composure a deep resentment smoldered within Addy's heart. A resentment that kept a firm barrier between them and surprisingly sent uncomfortable prickles of guilt rushing through him.

Even more surprising, he discovered himself regretting
the disturbing loss of Addy's infectious love for life. It was
one thing to request she behave in a manner befitting her
position and quite another to see her fading to a mere shadow
before his very eyes.

At last a soft knock on the door brought an end to his
dark thoughts. Glancing at the gilded clock on the mantel
he realized that it was precisely nine o'clock, the hour he
met with Addy each morning.

Although he suspected his wife considered their daily
meeting rather like a reluctant child forced to confront an
overbearing parent, he continued to insist she make an
appearance.

It was not that he desired to create further ill will between
them, he thought wearily. Heaven knew that he felt chilled
to the bone when she was near. But perhaps absurdly he
continued to hold the faint hope that they might eventually
establish a closer relationship.

Addy was his wife. For better or worse they were stuck
together. He did not believe he could endure fifty years of
their armed truce.

Smoothing his expression to polite lines he watched Addy
slip into the room and obediently move to settle in the chair
across the desk from him. This morning she was attired in
a dove gray gown with her hair ruthlessly pulled atop her
head. Only the heavy gold bracelet that encircled her wrist
added a dash of color, a bracelet that had been a gift from
her wretched father. He smothered a sigh at the pallor of
her lovely countenance and the unmistakable shadows
beneath the midnight black eyes.

Gads, to look at her one would presume he beat her at
least once a day.

"Good morning, Addy," he forced himself to murmur
in cool tones. "I hope that you slept well?"

She folded her hands in her lap and reluctantly met his gaze. "Quite well, thank you."

He studied how thin her countenance had become. "You appear somewhat pale. I hope that you have not caught a chill? The weather has been very unpredictable this spring."

She shrugged aside his concern. "My constitution has always been quite sturdy. 'Tis certain a few showers are not enough to make me ill."

He smiled with rueful humor. "Yes, I recall how you used to love walking in the rain. Usually barefoot with your hair hanging down your back."

"I was very much the hoyden when I was young," she retorted stiffly, as if presuming he were somehow censuring her youthful exuberance. "I assure you I no longer run through the rain with or without my shoes."

Adam's smile faltered. Blast it all. What did he have to do to soothe her prickly defenses?

"No, I realize that you have become all that is proper."

"That was what your requested, was it not?"

"So I did." He paused before leaning his arms upon the desk and regarding her with a growing sense of frustration. "I did not mean, however, that you were forced to become a mere ghost of yourself, nor that you imprison yourself in this townhouse. Do you have plans for today?"

Her chin tilted in a familiar defensive manner. "I shall go over the menu with Cook and see that the linens are aired."

"Such tasks can be easily put off," he retorted. "Surely you would prefer to go out?"

"Where would I go? I know few people in London."

"There are several places of interest. You could visit a few of the more notable sights. Tower of London. St. Paul's Cathedral. Or perhaps you would prefer an afternoon at the museum?"

"On my own?" she demanded. "That would surely look odd to the rest of society?"

Adam breathed out a harsh sigh. "You are right, of course," he acknowledged, knowing he had too readily used his duties with the War Department as an excuse to abandon his bride. In his defense, however, she did not bother to hide her preference for his absence from their home. "I shall arrange my schedule so that I will be free to accompany you later in the week. I have been quite remiss not to introduce you to a few ladies who would include you in their activities."

He had meant his words as an apology, but with a jerky motion Addy rose to her feet.

"That is not necessary, Adam. I realize you are very busy."

"Meaning you would prefer that I did not make the effort?"

"Meaning that I understand that you do not have the time." She conjured a cold smile. "Now, if you will excuse me I must speak with Mrs. Hall."

Adam opened his mouth to argue. Could she not bend even a little?

Then he gave a weary shake of his head. He had learned that pressing Addy only drove her further away.

"Of course. I shall see you at dinner."

He watched as she scurried from the room, then pulled his schedule toward him. He had wasted an entire morning on futile regrets. Until Addy chose to make an effort to respond to his tentative peace offerings there was nothing he could do.

In the meantime he had on his mind the thousands of soldiers who depended upon the efforts of the War Department to see them home safely. Such responsibility could not be taken lightly. It was his duty to do his job to the very best of his ability.

He swiftly finished the schedule and sifted through the morning's correspondence. At last satisfied that he had dealt with the most pressing details he meticulously cleared his desk. Storing away his quill he was abruptly interrupted when the thin, stiff-faced butler entered the library and offered a creaking bow.

"Pardon me, sir. A Vicar Humbly has requested to see you."

Adam felt a jolt of shock. Vicar Humbly? In London? Good God, he had known Humbly all his life. It was nearly inconceivable that the vague, rather unworldly Vicar would travel such a distance. He would wager his last quid the old man had not spent more than one night away from the Vicarage.

"Show him in, Chatson," he commanded.

"Very good."

Adam rose to his feet and walked round the desk as he awaited the arrival of Humbly. It had been months since he had last seen the old Vicar. Not since his wedding, he realized with a vague pang.

Within moments Chatson returned with a short, decidedly stout gentleman. Adam smiled at the rumpled black coat and wispy gray hairs that stood on end. Humbly always managed to appear as if he had just crawled from beneath a bush.

"Humbly. Welcome," Adam murmured, moving forward to shake hands with his unexpected guest.

"Thank you, Adam." Humbly flashed a sweet smile as he absently patted his crumpled cravat. "I hope I do not intrude?"

"Certainly not. Although I must confess this is an unexpected surprise."

A faintly befuddled expression crossed the Vicar's round countenance.

"Then you did not receive my note? How wretchedly

awkward. I was certain I had posted it before I left Surrey. Of course, the mail coach is never quite as predictable as one would hope. I must offer my apologies for descending upon you in such a fashion.''

Adam waved aside the rambling apology. To be honest, he was pleased to see his old friend. Despite Humbly's vague, rather foolish manner he possessed an odd ability to strike directly at the truth of a matter.

''Think nothing of it. I hope you intend to remain with us for a visit? I know Addy would be pleased to have a familiar face about.''

''Well, I should not wish to be a burden,'' the Vicar faintly protested. ''Although I have never married, I do know that newly wedded couples prefer their privacy.''

Adam gave an unwittingly revealing grimace. ''Do not fear, Humbly. Addy will be delighted to have a guest. Please, have a seat.''

With a rather searching gaze Humbly lowered his bulk onto a sturdy chair. Adam swiftly smoothed any expression from his features as he leaned against his desk.

''I hope you had a pleasant trip to town?''

''No, indeed. Quite ghastly. Not only did the coachman insist upon traveling at an indecent pace, he halted at the most wretched posting inn. I would swear the food had been found in a nearby gutter and on top of it all, I fear I somehow managed to lose my best hat and at least one of my cravats.'' He gave a sad shake of his head. ''I shall no doubt receive a dreadful scolding when I return to the Vicarage. Mrs. Stalwart does not seem to comprehend how difficult it is to keep one's things about one.''

Adam couldn't prevent a small chuckle as he thought of the formidable widow who ruled the Vicarage was well as poor Humbly.

''Perhaps you will have the opportunity to replace them while you are in town.''

The Vicar immediately cheered. "A capital notion. Yes, indeed. That is precisely what I shall do."

Adam tilted his head to one side. "Had I known you were coming to London I would have gladly sent my own carriage to fetch you. Is there a particular reason you came to town?"

"Oh, a bit of business with the Bishop." He waved a plump hand. "I am soon to retire, you know."

Adam felt a stab of shock. Brenville without Vicar Humbly? It was impossible to imagine.

"No, I did not know. It will be a sad loss."

The Vicar reddened with pleasure. "Thank you, Adam, but I am certain the new Vicar will be a blessing. He seems to be very energetic and quite determined to put the church in order. The dear Lord knows that I have never been very efficient with records and such. They are in sad disarray." The sherry brown eyes suddenly widened. "Come to think of it, he reminds me somewhat of you, Adam. Very practical and organized."

Adam abruptly stiffened, his features tight. "He has my sympathy."

"Eh?" Humbly blinked in surprise.

With a restless shrug Adam pushed himself from the desk and paced toward a window that overlooked the back garden.

"I have come to realize that I am a rather tedious fellow with all my practical notions and adherence to schedules."

"Nonsense," Humbly protested with gratifying sincerity. "You are a very responsible and worthy gentleman."

Adam studied the roses just coming into bloom. "Not all would think so."

"Well, we cannot please all of God's children," the Vicar said briskly.

The image of Addy's pale, unhappy face rose to his mind. "No, I suppose not."

As if able to read his very thoughts, Humbly cleared his throat. "Tell me how Addy is."

"She is well," he forced himself to say as he turned back to meet his guest's curious gaze.

"I suppose that she has taken London by storm? Such a charming and vibrant child."

"Actually we have not attended many social events. I have been quite occupied with my work."

The older man looked vaguely embarrassed, as if he sensed he had unknowingly pressed a tender nerve.

"Of course. You no doubt have little time to devote to such foolishness. Perfectly understandable."

"To tell the truth I have begun to consider the notion that I have been remiss in not introducing Addy to society," he confessed. "Your visit will be the perfect opportunity to correct my oversight."

"Oh, you mustn't change your schedule for me."

"It is a long overdue change," he assured Humbly. "I will speak with Liverpool. He will not be pleased, but I am certain they will muddle along just fine without my constant presence."

There was the sound of approaching footsteps then, the ever efficient housekeeper marched into the room to place a heavy tray upon a table near the Vicar.

"Here we are, sir," she said in cheerful tones. "I thought your guest might be in need of some refreshment."

"Thank you, Mrs. Hall. Will you inform my wife that we have a guest?"

"Of course."

With brisk motions the housekeeper left the room and Adam waved a hand toward the vast array of delicacies that filled the room with tantalizing aroma.

"Please help yourself, Humbly."

"Thank you. Perhaps I will have a cup of tea." Leaning forward, the Vicar poured a cup of tea then gave a sudden exclamation of delight. "Oh my, are those lemon tarts?"

Adam smiled. "Yes. And I can assure you that they are quite good."

"Lovely." Piling a plate with several of the tarts Humbly took a large bite and closed his eyes in pleasure. "Ah, yes. Delicious."

Adam politely remained silent as the Vicar indulged himself in the delicate pastries. It was clearly a treat for the older man.

It was several moments before Addy at last stepped through the door and regarded him with guarded puzzlement.

"You sent for me?"

"Yes." He moved to stand at her side. "As you can see we have a most welcome guest."

Turning her head she noted the plump gentleman struggling to his feet. A wide smile abruptly curved her lips as she rushed forward to give their guest a swift hug.

"Mr. Humbly."

"Addy, my dear. How delightful it is to see you again."

"This is a lovely surprise."

The older man gave a charming grimace. "Well, it was not intended to be a surprise at all, but once again my well-devised plans have gone awry. I can only pray that you will take pity upon an old vicar."

Addy gave a click of her tongue. "You must know you are always welcome here."

"How very kind." Stepping back Humbly studied the young woman in a thorough manner. "My, how very sophisticated you have become. Nothing at all like the gypsy who left Surrey."

Adam watched Addy stiffen at the soft words. "You must compliment Adam," she said in a low voice. "He chose my entire wardrobe."

Although Humbly could not have missed the sudden tension in the air, he merely smiled in his kindly way.

"Well, he always did possess exquisite taste, which he displayed when he chose you for a wife."

Addy's lips twisted. "Yes."

Unwilling to drag the poor Vicar into their marital woes, Adam abruptly stepped forward.

"I have been telling Humbly that we must find a means of keeping him entertained. Perhaps you will be so kind as to sort through our various invitations and select a few that our guest would enjoy?"

The dark gaze flashed in his direction with a measure of surprise. "I thought your schedule was too full to include invitations?"

"I will speak with Liverpool today. I am certain that I can manage an evening or two during the week."

There was a pause before she gave a shrug. "If you wish."

"Thank you." He turned to offer Humbly a bow. "I fear I must be on my way. I do hope you will make yourself at home."

"Yes, yes. Very kind," Humbly murmured.

Turning slightly he met his wife's narrowed gaze. "Addy, may I have a word?"

She gave a cool nod of her head. "Of course."

In silence she followed him from the room and down the stairs to the foyer. At last Adam halted to study Addy's pale countenance.

"I wished to assure myself that Humbly's visit will not be too taxing for you."

She blinked in genuine surprise at his soft question. "Of course not. I am delighted he has arrived."

"If you are certain. I could always put him up at a hotel."

She gave a firm shake of her head. "No. It will be nice to have someone about the house."

Adam could easily determine she was indeed pleased at the thought of Humbly's visit. There was a glow in the midnight eyes that he had not seen in far too long.

His hand rose to stroke the softness of her cheek only to drop at the realization she was more than likely to freeze at his touch rather than be comforted. He knew from bitter experience that she found their intimate relationship a mere duty to be endured with silent dignity.

"Addy, I realize that I have neglected you," he confessed in tight tones. "In truth I did not consider how isolated you would feel in London."

She lifted one shoulder. "You have been very busy."

"Yes. Perhaps too busy," he retorted in dry tones. Would things be different between Addy and himself if he hadn't succumbed to the pressures of the War Department? Impossible to say, he conceded with an unconscious shake of his head. "I will speak with Liverpool today."

"There is no need, Adam. I am certain that the Vicar and I can keep one another entertained."

His lips thinned with barely restrained annoyance. "I do not doubt that. Humbly has already accomplished what I have been striving to achieve for months."

Her expression was guarded. "What?"

"He has brought a smile to your face." He gave a stiff bow. "I will return for dinner."

Turning on his heel he snatched his hat and gloves from the side table and walked out the door.

For a gentleman who prided himself on his unshakable composure, he felt very much like putting his hand through a solid wall.

Addy remained standing in the foyer for a long moment after Adam's abrupt exit.

If she did not know better she would have thought Adam was angry when he left.

But that was impossible.

Adam was never angry.

He was always cool and detached and in utter command.

In the few months that they had been wed he had never once lost his temper or even raised his voice.

She had become convinced over the past weeks that he simply did not possess emotions. Or at the very least he kept them so deeply buried they had no opportunity to slip past his perfect composure.

A daunting realization for a woman of high spirits and volatile temperament.

Addy gave a restless shake of her head and she turned to make her way back up the stairs.

She had known when she wed Adam that he was a distant and aloof gentleman. She had also known that he deeply disapproved of her family. And her own unconventional manners.

She should have suspected that he would demand she conform to his rigid expectations. And that he would keep her very much in the background as he continued his life uninterrupted.

If only her father had not extravagantly squandered his fortune, she inwardly sighed. Or worse, borrowed so heavily against the expectation of her wedding to Adam.

If only . . .

Addy abruptly squashed the futile longings.

There were no if onlys. The fact was that she had no choice but to wed Adam. She could only try to make the best she could of the situation.

Smoothing her hands over the fine fabric of her gray skirt, Addy stepped back into the library. Now was not the time to fret over her marriage.

"Please have a seat," she said, smiling as she perched on a firm sofa. She was genuinely delighted that the Vicar had come for a visit. His sweet, kindly nature always managed to lift her spirits.

Regaining his seat, Mr. Humbly heaved a faint sigh. "I

do apologize for descending upon you in such a fashion. I can not think what happened to my letter.''

"Do not be silly. I am quite delighted you have come for a visit. You can catch me up on the gossip from home.''

He smiled gently. ''First I wish to know how you are doing, my dear.''

Addy could not prevent herself from growing rigid at his probing question.

"How could I be anything but happy?'' she at last managed in what she hoped was a flippant tone. ''I have several beautiful homes, ample staff, and a very generous allowance. Most women would be quite envious of my position.''

The steady brown gaze never wavered. ''You are not most women, Addy, and you have never cared for such nonsense. I have never seen you happier than standing before your easel covered in paint.''

Ridiculous tears pricked at her eyes and she swiftly lowered her thick lashes to hide her momentary weakness.

"As the wife of a consultant to the War Department it would not be proper to be covered in paint. I must think of my position.''

The bushy gray brows rose in surprise. ''You do not paint at all?''

"No.''

"Oh.'' He abruptly appeared crestfallen. ''How vastly disappointing.''

Addy was startled by his odd dismay. ''Why?''

"Well, I had hoped . . . no, forgive me. I am an old and silly man.''

Intrigued, Addy leaned forward. ''No, please tell me.''

The Vicar waved an embarrassed hand. ''It is no doubt a ridiculous tradition, but all the Vicars in Brenville have left behind a portrait in the Vicarage. I had hoped for your consent to do mine.''

Addy was caught off guard by his request. "But I only dabble in painting. I am certainly not trained to do portraits."

"Ah, but you have a unique talent given to you by God," he said firmly. "I would be deeply honored if you would agree."

Oddly touched by his obvious faith in her dubious talent Addy blushed in confusion.

"Oh, I do not know."

"Please, Addy." He regarded her with a coaxing expression. "I could not bear to go to some stranger who might very well feel compelled to add a bit of dignity to this very plain countenance or pose me in a ridiculous manner. I merely desire a simple portrait by someone I trust."

Addy began to waver. Until this moment she had not realized just how much she had missed her painting.

"I suppose I could do a few sketches to see if there is one you desire."

"Lovely." The older man settled back in his seat. "You have deeply relieved my mind."

"You have yet to see my work," she warned.

"I trust you completely."

Her heart warmed at his words. "Thank you."

"Now, let me tell you of the neighborhood." He absently reached for a lemon tart and took a healthy bite. "Squire Blackwell is still courting maidens half his age and refuses to accept the lures of poor Widow Connell who is desperate to wed well. The doctor shocked everyone and eloped with the baker's daughter. Of course you know that both Beatrice and Victoria have recently wed."

Addy thought whimsically of her childhood friends. Odd to think of them now married. Almost as odd as thinking of herself as married.

"Yes. How are they?"

The shaggy brows drew together as he pondered her question. "In truth I fear they are both having their difficulties in settling down to wedded life. I believe the first few months of marriage are always somewhat difficult.''

Her lips twisted in a wry smile. Difficult was a decided understatement.

"Yes."

" 'The Lord is near to the brokenhearted and saves the crushed in spirit,' " the Vicar quoted softly, his gaze oddly understanding. "All will be well, my dear." With an awkward motion he rose to his feet, surprisingly stuffing the half-eaten tart into the pocket of his coat. "Now, if you will excuse me I believe I shall seek my room and have a bit of rest."

Addy readily stood and moved to link her arm with her guest. She smiled as she realized the vast townhouse suddenly did not seem so empty anymore.

"Certainly. I shall show you the way."

Chapter Two

Adam arrived back at the townhouse in ample time to change into an elegant black evening coat and pantaloons. As always he insisted upon tying his own cravat while his valet watched with pained martyrdom. He refused to be swayed into the latest fashion of high shirt points and cravats so large a gentleman could not turn his head. A simple elegance was far more commanding than silly knots and bows.

He did allow the servant to brush his dark hair toward his lean countenance and to ensure that not the tiniest speck marred the perfection of his attire. Then, with only a passing glance in the pier mirror, he let himself out of his chambers and headed down to the front salon.

Entering the room, he took a moment to appreciate the classical lines of the rosewood furnishings and the soothing pale green satin wallcoverings. There were several delightful Wedgwood pieces upon the various tables and a carved marble chimneypiece with a portrait of his parents hanging above it.

His father had possessed unerring taste in furnishing his homes and Adam had never considered the notion of changing the décor once he had taken possession of the houschold. In all honesty he spent so little time in the house there had been no overwhelming urge to place his own stamp upon the surroundings.

Not certain where that odd thought had come from, Adam turned to discover the Vicar standing beside the fire sipping the fine brandy Adam kept readily stocked.

"Good evening, Humbly."

The older man smiled with warm welcome. Although he had obviously changed for dinner he still managed to look rumpled with his hair sticking upward with tenacious independence.

"Welcome home, Adam."

"Is Addy not down yet?"

"No, I fear that we lost track of time," he admitted ruefully. "She went to change only a few moments ago."

Adam smiled somewhat wryly. "I suppose I may reasonably surmise that you had an enjoyable afternoon?"

The sherry eyes twinkled. "Yes, indeed. I hope you do not mind, but I have asked Addy to paint my portrait. She has been sketching me all afternoon."

Adam felt a flicker of surprise. He could not recall the last occasion he had seen Addy with her paints. Certainly not since their wedding. A disturbing image of Addy standing in a field with the wind whipping her brilliant skirts and her raven locks tumbled about her shoulders rose to mind. How often had he watched her from afar? Not daring to approach for fear that she might flutter away like a frightened butterfly.

With an effort he banished the image. Such days were in the past and best forgotten.

"No, I am delighted," he retorted in all truth. "I do not believe she has painted in some time."

"Ah well, I believe she feared that it would not be entirely seemly for the wife of a War Department consultant to be splattered with paint," Humbly said in vague tones.

Adam grimaced, moving to pour himself a measure of brandy. "Yet another sin laid upon my doorstep," he muttered.

"I beg your pardon?"

Adam slowly turned back to face the Vicar. Humbly could not remain at the townhouse and not realize that all was not well between him and Addy, he ruefully acknowledged. Perhaps it would be best to simply confess the truth.

"Do you know, Humbly, I have always possessed a great deal of arrogance regarding my own infallibility," he said, leaning against the heavy side table. "I believed that if I set upon a task with the proper knowledge and a careful strategy I would be assured of success."

Humbly shrugged. "It is a reasonable assumption."

"Not when it comes to marriage," he retorted grimly.

A hint of sympathy touched the plump countenance. "Is there something troubling you, my son?"

Adam abruptly dropped his gaze to the amber liquid in his glass. He was never comfortable discussing his inner thoughts and feelings. He had been taught from a young age that a man was expected to remain stoically in command at all times.

"When my father informed me of my grandfather's promise to wed me to Addy I was frankly horrified. The Morrow household is closer to an asylum than a respectable home. Addy's mother is forever painting naked footmen, farmers, and even aristocrats in her front salon and her father is a notorious rogue who has managed to create scandal from Surrey to London to Devonshire. That isn't even to mention the unsavory characters that are constantly clinging to their household. Revolutionaries, drunken poets, and debauched dandies without a feather to fly with.''

Humbly cleared his throat in an uncomfortable manner. ''Yes, the Morrows are rather eccentric.''

''Eccentric?'' Adam gave a humorless laugh. ''Gads, Morrow keeps a string of mistresses in a cottage just a few paces from his own home.''

''Very unpleasant.''

''And, then, Addy.'' Adam heaved an unconscious sigh, feeling the familiar tangle of fondness, exasperation, and guilt that wracked him whenever he thought of his young wife. ''Well, she was hardly the placid debutante I had thought to make my wife. She was wild, headstrong, and utterly lacking in fashionable polish.''

The Vicar was swift to bristle at the least hint of censure toward his beloved friend.

''It is true that Addy is not sophisticated, but she has always possessed a good heart and lovely spirit.''

''Yes, which I assured myself would be admirable qualities in a wife if I could ensure she did not follow in her family's footsteps,'' he said, taking a sudden gulp of the fiery liquid.

''Obviously she has not,'' Humbly pointed out in reasonable tones.

Adam winced in spite of himself. ''No, I made very certain before we wed that she understood I would not tolerate the scandalous behavior of her parents,'' he admitted. ''I made a precise list of what I expected in my bride. I even chose her wardrobe to ensure she would not be an embarrassment when we arrived in London.''

A heavy silence greeted his dark words and, glancing upward, Adam discovered Humbly regarding him with a watchful gaze.

''And Addy agreed to this list?'' he at last demanded in carefully bland tones.

Adam waved a restless hand. "What choice did she have? Her parents had managed to squander their fortune years ago and only survived in the knowledge they would receive a settlement when Addy and I wed."

"Ah." The Vicar nodded in a knowing manner. "Well, you should be pleased. Addy has become a most proper lady."

"Yes, I should be delighted," Adam agreed grimly.

"But you are not?"

Adam polished off the brandy in a single gulp. He thought of the past few months with Addy in his home. No, he was not bloody well delighted. No man would be delighted to possess a shadow that slipped from his grasp whenever he reached out to take hold.

"It is not pleasant to live with a woman who is clearly miserable," he conceded with a pained grimace.

"Surely you exaggerate," Humbly protested.

Adam gave a shake of his head. "No, I do not. Since becoming my wife Addy has lost her spirit. She no longer laughs or teases with others. Indeed, she does not take any pleasure whatsoever in our lives."

"Well, she is in London for the first time with few friends about," the Vicar attempted to comfort him. "She is no doubt lonely."

Adam desperately wished that loneliness were all that troubled his bride. Such a trifling problem would be easy to solve. He knew all too well that her distress ran far deeper.

"I have offered to make more time together, but she has made it clear that she does not seek my company. The truth is that she barely tolerates my presence."

Humbly gave a click of his tongue, oddly not shocked or embarrassed by Adam's uncomfortable confession.

"I am sure you are mistaken, Adam," he said firmly. "Perhaps she merely fears that she cannot please you."

Adam frowned at the accusation. He was intimately familiar with a fear of not being able to please a demanding taskmaster. His own father had been a stern man who demanded nothing short of perfection from his only son. Adam had struggled most of his life to live up to such impossible expectations, up until the day his father had at last been laid to rest in the family crypt.

Could he have unintentionally made Addy fear he intended to be forever critical? Could she be avoiding him because she thought he was judging her and finding her lacking?

It was an unpleasant thought. And one he did not wish to dwell upon until he possessed the proper privacy to give it his full attention.

Giving a shake of his head Adam set aside his empty glass. "Forgive me, Humbly. I did not mean to burden you with my troubles. Especially when you have just arrived."

His guest smiled with gentle understanding. "It is what I do. You may always confide in me, Adam. I hope that you consider me your friend."

"Thank you."

The distant sound of approaching footsteps brought an end to any further conversation. Adam squared his shoulders as he prepared to meet his wife's cool gaze, but oddly, Humbly began to pat his coat pockets in a distracted manner.

"Oh dear."

"Is something the matter?"

"I believe I have left my watch in the library," he muttered. "I shall return in a moment."

With surprising speed the Vicar waddled across the room and disappeared through a side door. Adam gave a shake of his head, suddenly realizing that he had been depending upon Humbly's bright chatter to fill the icy distance between him and his wife.

There was no help for it, however, as Addy stepped into the room, attired in a pale lavender gown. He winced slightly at the unbecoming knot of curls scraped to the top of her head before offering a half bow.

"Good evening, Addy." He slowly straightened. "Would you care for a ratafia?"

"Yes, thank you." She waited until he crossed to hand her a thin, crystal glass. "I am sorry I am late."

"Humbly has already explained your absence. Besides, I assure you that it was worth the wait," he said gallantly, unsurprised when she shifted with unease.

She was unaccustomed to compliments from him.

"Where is Mr. Humbly?"

"I believe he went in search of an errant watch." Adam returned to his post beside the side table. It was that or lift his hands and wrench her raven curls free of the painful knot. "The Vicar tells me that you have agreed to paint his portrait."

"Oh, no." She gave a sharp shake of her head. "I have only agreed to make a few sketches. I do not feel qualified to paint a portrait."

"Nonsense. You possess an exquisite talent," he insisted.

"We shall see." She flashed him a wary glance. "Unless, of course, you are opposed to the notion?"

His brows drew together at her question. "Why the devil should I be opposed?"

"It is not the occupation of most ladies of society."

"Addy, I would be quite happy to know you are doing something that pleases you," he said in tones he hoped were reassuring. In truth he wanted to throw up his hands in annoyance. "I am not the ogre that you have made me out to be."

Her lashes abruptly dropped. "It is difficult to know what you will or will not approve of, Adam."

Adam resisted the urge to check and see if he had sprouted horns and a tail.

Surely only a devil could be as bad as Addy believed?

"For God's sake, Addy, all I have ever requested was that you not create a scandal. Surely that is not unreasonable considering the circumstances?" he demanded in a tight voice.

"Considering what circumstances?" she asked, her magnificent eyes flashing with a sudden fire. "My family?"

"Well, they are hardly respectable," he ground out.

"Perhaps not, but they do know how to enjoy life."

"Oh yes, they know how to enjoy it all right. With every scoundrel and misfit who happens by," he muttered.

"Surely that is preferable to a tedious existence where one is constantly obliged to fear what others are saying about one?"

The unfair accusation stirred Adam's rare temper. "I see. You would not then be adverse to having me devote my life to cards and mistresses while our neighbors twitter behind your back?" he requested coldly.

A faint hint of color touched her cheeks. "Do you think they do not twitter at the knowledge you prefer to ignore your bride in favor of your musty books and the War Department?"

Adam was taken aback by her fierce words. "Addy . . ."

He did not know precisely what he intended to say and actually it did not matter as Humbly chose that moment to return to the room with his bright smile.

"Here were are. I hope I have not kept dinner waiting?"

"Not at all." Moving toward the Vicar, Addy linked her arm through his. "Shall we go through?"

Together they left the room, leaving Adam to follow behind.

Glancing up at the lovely fresco painted on the ceiling, Adam grimly restored his composure. He would not be goaded into fleeing to the peace of his club. Addy had won that game on too many occasions.

Although Addy had never truly felt herself a wife, she did take a quiet pride in running the household with a smooth efficiency.

Unlike her own mother who hired and fired staff on a whim, usually depending upon her need for models in her paintings, Addy had servants who had worked for the Drake family for years. It was more than a little intimidating when she had first arrived. What did a green country girl know of running a London establishment? But with the knowledge that the rather arrogant staff would be swift to take advantage of any scent of uncertainty, she had forced herself to take firm command.

In time she had gained obedience and at last respect from the servants. Even from the temperamental cook who notoriously disliked interference in her sacred domain.

Now as she watched Mr. Humbly sit back and pat his considerable stomach she felt a measure of satisfaction. She need have no fear her household would fail to provide every comfort to even an unexpected guest.

"Delicious," the Vicar said with a heartfelt sigh. "Truly the duck was a masterpiece."

"I shall convey your appreciation to Cook," Addy retorted, rising smoothly to her feet. "If you will excuse me I will leave you to your port."

Without warning Adam rose to his feet with a shake of his head. "Nonsense. We shall join you in the salon if Humbly does not mind?"

"Not at all," Humbly denied. "I never much cared for port."

"I recall that you do possess a fondness for brandy," Adam said with a smile.

"Ah well, we must all have our small sins," Humbly confessed as he struggled to his feet.

"Yes." Adam's lips twisted as he politely moved to offer Addy his arm.

With no choice Addy lightly placed her hand upon his forearm. Although they had been wed for months she had never entirely become accustomed to having his large male form near. Not even when he sought her bed in the shadows of the night. That no doubt accounted for the manner in which she instinctively stiffened as the heat and spicy scent wrapped about her. She felt almost smothered by the sheer force of his presence.

They traveled the short distance in silence, then, leaving Addy beside the fire, Adam moved to pour two generous dashes of brandy for himself and their guest.

Accepting his glass Humbly glanced about the room with an expression of contentment.

"What a lovely home this is," he said in satisfaction. "I can not say that I care for the new fashion of lacquer and heavy oriental draperies. Nothing quite so comforting as solid English furnishings, do you not think, my dear?"

Addy forced a smile. She could hardly confess that she had never dared to suggest the house be altered in any way.

"Oh yes, it is very comforting."

"And such a pleasant location," the Vicar continued. "With a park just around the corner, one would not miss the country quite so much."

"Perhaps we shall take a stroll there tomorrow," Addy suggested.

"A lovely notion."

"I thought you were to meet with the Bishop?" Adam abruptly intruded into the conversation, his tone oddly sharp.

Humbly waved a dismissive hand. "Plenty of time for such business. I far prefer strolling through the park with a beautiful maiden than debating theology with the Bishop in his stuffy office.''

The lean countenance seemed to darken. ''Of course.''

''Perhaps you would care to join us, Adam?'' the Vicar generously offered.

''I fear that I have scheduled several meetings for tomorrow.''

A ridiculous pang of disappointment flared through Addy. Ridiculous, because she had known when she had wed Adam that she was no more than a necessary duty to him.

''You will discover, Mr. Humbly, that my husband is a great believer in scheduling meetings,'' she retorted with a hint of tartness.

Adam thinned his lips at the deliberate barb. ''I merely prefer an orderly existence. Unlike most of the ton I have no desire to lay indolently in bed through the greater part of the day only to rise and dash about town in search of the latest gossip or flirtation.''

''Oh, yes. Such foolishness,'' Mr. Humbly murmured.

Addy met the gray gaze without flinching. ''They seem to enjoy their frivolous pursuits.''

''Because they have nothing more substantial to fill their time. It is a pity more do not use their intellect upon occasion.''

''There is nothing wrong with enjoying oneself upon occasion,'' she perversely argued. ''Life can be very dreary without some excitement.''

He regarded her for a long moment then he gave a slow, rather weary nod of his head.

''No doubt you are correct, my dear. If you will excuse me I believe I will retire. It has been a rather trying day.''

With a correct bow Adam moved across the room and disappeared through the doorway.

Addy discovered herself biting her lower lip, suddenly wishing that she had kept her hasty words to herself. Just

for a moment she thought that she might have glimpsed
something that was very close to pain in Adam's smoky
eyes.

Disconcerted, she stared at the empty doorway, wondering
if it was at all possible that her husband did indeed possess
more than a schedule book where his heart should be. Then,
realizing that Humbly was regarding her with a watchful
gaze she hurried to fill the tense silence.

"Adam possesses a dislike for frivolity, I fear," she said
in what she hoped was light tones.

Humbly's expression became somber. "It is not really
surprising. His father was a very stern gentleman who
demanded perfection from his only son. Adam was expected
to assume responsibility from his earliest childhood. A pity,
really. He has been given little joy in his life."

Addy gave a restless shrug, not wishing to acknowledge
the pang within her heart.

"His father died years ago."

"Yes, but he is still attempting to please him, even if he
does not realize it," the Vicar said softly. "It is odd, but
sons never quite rid themselves of the need to seek their
father's approval. Especially when it has been withheld.
Now, I believe I shall also seek my bed. I am unaccustomed
to travel and I fear that my old bones are beginning to
protest."

"Of course." Addy gave a vague smile. "I shall have
breakfast sent to your room."

"Thank you, my dear. Sleep well."

With a nod the Vicar ambled from the room, leaving
behind a disturbed Addy.

He has been given little joy in his life.

The words echoed painfully through her mind.

Absurd, of course.

Adam had never sought joy from her.

He had requested she be a proper, undemanding wife.

She had done her best to be that wife. Even at the sacrifice of her own happiness.

She had no reason to feel that renegade prick of guilt.

No reason at all.

Chapter Three

Vicar Humbly was frankly miserable.

Although the vast townhouse in the fashionable neighborhood of Mayfair was no doubt lovely with its crimson and gold décor and heavily gilded trim, at the moment it was unbearably crowded with a crush of elegant guests.

Mopping his head with a large handkerchief, Humbly briefly longed for the quiet peace of his Vicarage. At such a late hour he would be cozily ensconced in his chair beside a lovely fire. No doubt he would be reading from his well-worn Bible while sipping a little of the brandy he kept cleverly hidden from Mrs. Stalwart's sharp eyes.

Precisely the manner in which he preferred to spend his evenings.

Instead he was being rudely jostled and occasionally elbowed as the guests surged about in an effort to find their friends or merely the best position in the room to show off their finery.

The Vicar sighed.

There would no doubt be several more such evenings to be endured before he accomplished his goal, he predicted ruefully.

Adam and Addy were in even more danger than he had feared.

Adam was too proud to admit that he had been wrong to try to change his wife into an image of his own making. And too unyielding to realize that it was precisely Addy's warm vivacity that he needed in his life.

And poor Addy was too resentful at being forced into a marriage with a man she thought cold and indifferent to realize the dependable worth of her husband.

Neither seemed willing to be first in offering the hand of peace.

Putting aside the futile desire to be home in Surrey, Humbly glanced at the gentleman at his side.

He sighed again at the cold, disapproving expression upon Adam's handsome countenance.

If the Vicar had hoped that time spent among the glittering gaiety of others would ease the tension between the two, he was doomed to disappointment.

Rather than enjoying the festivities together, Adam had stoically remained in the shadows while Addy had allowed herself to be swept away by a series of charming rogues.

It was all enough to make even the most kindly tempered vicar mutter a curse beneath his breath.

"Gracious, it is very warm, is it not?" he at last shouted above the din, hoping to ease the tension he could feel radiating from Adam's large form.

"Smothering," the younger man agreed.

"Do you think they will open a door or two?"

"Not likely." Adam shot him a wry glance. "A hostess can not consider her party a success without at least one maiden fainting in the crush."

Humbly wiped the moisture from his forehead. "An unpleasant notion."

"Yes." Adam's gaze shifted as a new wave of guests pressed through the doorway. "Humbly, I should move back if I were you."

"What?" Humbly leaned forward in an effort to hear his companion's low warning then he gave a sharp howl as a large matron with a hideous yellow gown stomped directly upon his foot. "Ye-ow."

Adam's lips twitched. "One of the numerous dangers of society," he drawled. "Never be in the path of a Marriage Minded Mama."

Humbly wiggled his toes, thankful to discover none were actually broken. "There are more dangers?"

Adam shrugged. "Well, to begin with you must never linger near a gentleman in his cups because he will invariably spill whatever he is drinking upon your coat. And if you must dance, take care to avoid the candle grease, which can create a challenge to the most graceful sportsman. Oh, and beware of Lady Stopel, who is a consummate pickpocket."

Humbly gave a choked sound of disbelief, quite certain he had misheard.

"A pickpocket?"

"Yes."

"You must be jesting?"

"Not at all," Adam insisted. "She is quite talented and generally manages to lift a half a dozen purses during the course of an evening. Her niece, however, is quite dependable in returning the stolen items the next morning."

Humbly gave a click of his tongue. Oppressive heat. An aching head. Near broken toes. And now fear for his meager purse.

"I begin to comprehend why you avoid such evenings," he mourned.

"I will admit that I far prefer a quiet evening at my club."

Humbly abruptly bit his tongue. Fool. He was suppose to be encouraging Adam to indulge his bride's love for frivolous enjoyment, not encouraging him to disappear to his club.

"At least Addy appears to be enjoying herself," he said brightly.

Adam abruptly shifted his gaze to his bride, who was currently chatting with a tall, bronze-haired gentleman.

"Yes."

Humbly felt a flicker of recognition at the sight of the gentleman's overly handsome features and lavish elegance.

"Who is that gentleman she is speaking with?"

"Lord Barclay," Adam retorted in clipped tones.

"He seems oddly familiar."

"He visited the Morrows last year." Adam's expression became even more grim as the handsome gentleman leaned close to Addy to whisper in her ear. "He is a notorious rake and fribble. I shall have to speak with Addy. I do not desire her to encourage such a connection."

Humbly's heart sank. Dear heavens, how could such an intelligent man be so completely lacking in sense when it came to his wife?

"I do not think a harmless encounter at a crowded ball is encouraging a connection," he protested.

Unswayed, Adam thinned his lips to a dangerous line. "Addy is very innocent and not accustomed to the nasty games that such men enjoy playing. She might very well plunge into disaster without realizing the danger."

Humbly thought it was far more likely this annoyingly stubborn gentleman at his side was about to blunder into disaster.

Could he not realize that he had done enough damage with his absurd lectures?

"Addy has always been very intelligent," he said sternly. "I do not believe she will seek out scandal."

"And what of excitement?" Adam demanded, a hint of bitterness entering his tone. "Surely you have realized that my wife is bored and restless in her marriage?"

"It is a very different life from what she was accustomed to."

"A fact that I absurdly presumed would please her."

Humbly abruptly stilled. He too had hoped that Addy would appreciate the solid security of her new life with Adam. He knew, after all, that she had not always approved of her parents' outlandish habits. There had even been times when he had discovered her crying over one of their more scandalous exploits.

But instead, she had come to feel trapped and smothered in her relationship with her husband. And, of course, resentful at being forced into marriage in the first place. She seemed to have forgotten the pain and uncertainty that could be caused by those who lived lives of frivolous indifference.

Perhaps it was time she be reminded that it was not utterly horrid to possess a husband who was dependable.

Humbly summoned the sweet smile that so effectively hid his devious intent.

"A young woman's or even a young man's fancy is rarely taken by what is best for her or him," he said with a lift of his hands. "Surely you have at one time or another been drawn to glitter rather than worth?"

He gave a restless shrug, no doubt recalling the lures of a pretty actress or a night devoted to cards and drink.

"Perhaps. But I have long since outgrown such nonsense."

"As will Addy."

The gray eyes abruptly narrowed. "Are you saying that I must be patient?"

"Yes, patience is always a most admirable trait," Humbly agreed slowly. "Of course, there is also something to be said for carpe diem."

"Seize the day?"

The Vicar gave a self-conscious cough. "It is just a fanciful thought, but perhaps Addy would be more content in her marriage if she were to discover that shallow impulsiveness is a poor substitute for true dependability."

Adam blinked in confusion. "What?"

Knowing he dare not press too far too quickly, he gave a vague shake of his head. "Nothing, nothing. As I said, I am a foolish old man, prone to fancies." His eyes widened as he glanced across the room at the bizarrely attired matron with something ominously hairy perched upon her shoulder. "Dear heavens, is that a monkey?"

Addy was thoroughly enjoying her evening.

It had been so very long since she had been among society. To dance, to laugh, to have handsome gentlemen flutter about her soothed a pride that had been battered by Adam's constant disapproval.

For the first time in ages she felt able to loosen her constraints and truly enjoy herself. Tomorrow, she defiantly decided, would take care of itself. For this one evening she would soak up all the excitement she had so missed since becoming Mrs. Drake.

With that thought in mind she regarded the handsome Lord Barclay who had efficiently maneuvered them to a shadowed corner. During his brief visit to Surrey the year before he had proven to be a charming companion. Tonight he was positively dazzling.

As if noting the hectic glitter in her eyes, Barclay smiled down at her upturned countenance.

"Are you warm?"

"It is rather stuffy," she agreed.

"Allow me." With an elegant motion the Lord removed the fan tied about her wrist and began to waft it before her in an effort to cool her heated cheeks.

"Thank you."

"It is my deepest pleasure to be of service, my dear," the gallant gentleman retorted. "After waiting for nearly a year to see you again I had almost given up hope."

Well acquainted with such banter, Addy gave a small laugh. "Fah. You never gave me a second thought after you left Surrey."

"That could not be further from the truth. You have haunted me since I first captured sight of you." His gaze boldly roamed over her tidy curls and modest yellow gown. "Of course, I must say that I far preferred your previous style of bright colors and your hair loose about your shoulders. There was something very natural and free about you."

She gave a faint shrug. "I am a proper married lady now."

"Do not remind me." He gave a dramatic shudder. "It breaks my heart to think of you tied to that pompous prig."

Her eyes widened at his unexpected words. "Lord Barclay!"

Her companion was clearly unrepentant. "It is true. He might possess a fortune, but he has no heart. He thinks of nothing but dreary duty."

Although it was no different from what she herself had thought, Addy found herself stiffening in protest.

"He is very kind to me," she felt compelled to point out.

Lord Barclay gave a click of his tongue. "He is no doubt kind to his dogs as well. A wife should be cherished and indulged."

She met his gaze squarely. "How do you know that I am not?"

"A woman well satisfied with her husband has a glow about her. You are distinctly lacking that glow."

Addy discovered she did not particularly care to have others speculating on the intimate state of her marriage.

"You are being absurd."

He stepped closer, a faint smile curving his full lips.

"No, I am being honest. Does that trouble you?"

"I am more baffled by your inordinate interest in my marriage," she retorted.

"Because I desire to see that happy child I once knew. It is a crime to have stolen your spirit."

Her brows drew together in a silent warning. "My spirit is my own. It cannot be stolen by anyone."

Far too wily not to realize that he had unwittingly overstepped his bounds, Lord Barclay gave a lighthearted chuckle.

"I cannot tell you how pleased I am to hear that, my dear."

She gave a wry shake of her head. "You, sir, are a very dangerous gentleman."

"Ah, but what is life without the spice of danger?"

"Safe?"

"Safe? Bah. A vastly overrated sentiment. Not to mention extraordinarily dull." He flashed her a knowing glance. "A woman such as yourself would never be content with such an existence."

She arched a raven brow. "And how could you presume to know?"

"Because I can see the restless dissatisfaction smoldering in those beautiful eyes." His voice lowered to a husky promise. "It makes me long to see them dark and sated with pleasure."

A prickle of alarm made Addy take a sudden step backward. A harmless bit of flirting was one thing. She had no intention of allowing him to believe she was interested in anything further.

"I believe we should change the conversation, my lord."

His gaze narrowed. "Do not tell me you are frightened?"

Addy reached out to firmly reclaim her fan. "I am sensible enough to know you are a reprehensible rake! If you wish to polish your fatal charms you should choose a more gullible victim."

"You have it wrong," he protested. "I have been felled by your beauty."

She rolled her eyes heavenward, but before she could take him to task for his foolishness, a sudden shadow fell over her.

A familiar tingle of awareness rushed through her and slowly she turned to confront the glittering gaze of her husband.

Her heart sank at the sight of his tight features and the grim line of his mouth.

Clearly he was once again annoyed with her behavior and anxious to offer her a reprimand.

Ignoring the gentleman who was regarding him with a lazy nonchalance, Adam held out his arm for her.

"My dance, I believe, my dear," he said in tones that warned he would tolerate no mutiny.

"Good Lord, you surely do not mean to dance with your own wife?" Lord Barclay mocked, even as Addy obediently laid her hand upon Adam's arm.

She felt her husband's muscles tense as he turned to regard the dandy with a scathing dislike.

"I hardly believe my choice in dancing partners is your concern, Barclay."

Barclay deliberately allowed his gaze to move to Addy's flushed countenance.

"On the contrary, it is the concern of every poor wretch in London. It is bad enough that you have wed the most enchanting creature in England and kept her secluded from society. To monopolize her on the one occasion she is allowed to make an appearance is positively Gothic."

Addy gritted her teeth as she realized the fair-haired devil was deliberately baiting Adam.

"It is a husband's prerogative to monopolize his wife if he so desires," Adam retorted in blighting tones.

Lord Barclay merely chuckled with a smug self-assurance. "Perhaps your wife might feel otherwise. Addy and I were enjoying a most intriguing discussion."

Addy could have stamped her foot in annoyance. The two men had clearly forgotten her presence in their bristling male need to best one another. Like two dogs fighting over a stray bone, she thought in disgust.

"I suggest that you limit your discussions with Mrs. Drake to the weather, Barclay," Adam warned, his cold control far more intimidating than any fiery display of temper.

Lord Barclay lifted a golden brow. "Is that a threat?"

"Obviously you are not as stupid as I feared." Having delivered his final shot, Adam swept Addy through the crowd and onto a darkened terrace.

Once alone with her husband, Addy turned to meet his cold glare with a flare of irritation. She did not care to be hauled from the party like a naughty child.

"There was no need to threaten Lord Barclay, Adam. We were merely sharing a polite conversation."

His jaw tightened in an ominous manner. Standing in the shadows he appeared larger and more intimidating than usual.

"Do not concern yourself, my dear. Barclay and I understand one another quite well."

Meaning that he had already decided that there could be nothing innocent between her and the dashing Lord, she thought wearily. Just another reminder that he would never fully trust her.

"I suppose you are angry," she said in dull tones.

The gray gaze became suddenly watchful. "What would make you think such a thing?"

"You have the expression upon your countenance that you wear when you are about to give me a lecture."

Adam appeared startled by her accusation. "Gads, am I truly so overbearing, Addy?"

She restlessly moved to the edge of the terrace, blindly staring at the shadowed garden beyond.

"You can be very stern."

"And you would prefer that I be more like Barclay?" he demanded in tight tones.

Addy gave a slow shake of her head. It was impossible to imagine Adam ever being lighthearted and charming. It simply was not a part of his nature.

"This is hardly the place to discuss our marriage, Adam."

She heard him move to stand directly behind her. Those faint tingles raced through her body as she felt his male heat sear through her satin gown.

"He is an arrogant lecher, Addy, who has ruined more than one maiden," he said with obvious impatience.

Addy reached out to grasp the stone railing. Once again he had managed to misunderstand the source of her irritation.

"And you believe me foolish enough to fall for his practiced charms?" she demanded. "Or perhaps you simply presume that because of my family I am incapable of being trusted?"

She heard him suck in a sharp breath. "Do not put words into my mouth."

"Can you deny that you do not wholly trust me, Adam?"

There was a long, tension-fraught silence during which Addy could hear the uneven beat of her heart.

"You make it very difficult," he at last confessed reluctantly.

"Difficult?" She abruptly turned to glare at him in rising anger. How dare he blame her for his lack of trust? "*I* make it difficult?"

The lean features were closed and impossible to read in the dim light.

"I am well aware, Addy, that you have not fully committed yourself to this marriage."

Addy's hands clenched at her side at the unfairness of it all.

"Are you mad?" she hissed, her eyes flashing with fury. "I have done nothing but commit myself. I live in your house, I wear the clothes you chose, follow your damnable schedule, and allow you into my bed. What more could you possibly ask of me?"

He seemed to flinch at her words, but the handsome features remained set in stern lines.

"I did not desire a martyr when I wed. I desired a wife. I assure you, there is no pleasure in watching your tragic form floating about the house or to know I am merely endured for the sake of duty in your bed. Is it any wonder that I prefer the comfort of my club to the coldness of my own home?"

Addy felt as if she had just been slapped. Never before had Adam spoken to her in such a manner and she found her heart clenching with an unexplainable pain.

"Perhaps you would prefer I return to Surrey?" she whispered in low tones.

The gray eyes flashed with an indefinable emotion. "You will remain in London, Addy. Make no mistake about that."

Feeling suddenly tired and unable to return to the gaiety of the ball, Addy lifted a hand to her throbbing temple.

"I think I shall return home," she muttered.

"Addy . . ."

"Please, Adam, I have the headache," she interrupted sharply.

He regarded her for a long moment before giving a resigned nod of his head.

"Very well. I shall locate Humbly."

Chapter Four

"No, you must not move," Addy commanded as the Vicar cast a languishing glance toward the tea tray that had been delivered by Mrs. Hall.

With a covert motion Mr. Humbly returned his head to the dignified angle that Addy had insisted upon.

"My dear Addy, I do not believe I could move if I wished to," he shamelessly lied. "I fear I have forever stiffened in this hideously uncomfortable position."

"Fah," she retorted with a decided lack of sympathy. Her hand moved swiftly as she sketched the prominent thrust of his nose. Much to her surprise, she had discovered she thoroughly enjoyed capturing the unique spirit of the Vicar in her numerous drawings. It was a true challenge to her skills. "I distinctly saw you glance longingly at those lemon tarts on the tray that Mrs. Hall just left sitting on the table."

Humbly heaved a long suffering sigh. "Well, it does seem a sin to allow such delectable creations to go to waste."

"They will not disappear in the next twenty minutes," she said dryly.

"Twenty minutes? Dear heavens, I shall expire."

Addy gave a reluctant chuckle at his fervent exclamation. Somehow this dear man always managed to lighten her mood. Not an easy task today.

After a near sleepless night she had awakened with a heavy spirit. She had been so determined to enjoy her evening at the ball. It was the first occasion she had had since her marriage to mingle with society. The first occasion to recall the pleasure of laughter and dancing.

But it had all gone horribly wrong.

Her jaw tightened as she recalled the manner with which Adam had hustled her from the ballroom like a disobedient child and proceeded to lecture her on a harmless conversation with Lord Barclay.

He had thoroughly ruined her evening and worse, he had wounded her pride with his blunt confession he did not trust her.

Dash it all. It had been uncomfortable enough living with Adam in a state of polite, frozen courtesy. She might have disliked guarding her every word and being abandoned for hours in this great tomb of a house, but at least she did not have to worry over sudden squabbles and sharp words that seemed to cut to her very soul.

Realizing that the Vicar was watching her with a hopeful expression she reluctantly set aside her drawing pad.

"Very well, we shall take a brief rest. A very brief rest," she warned as she moved to pour her guest a cup of tea and place several lemon tarts upon a plate.

Joining her upon the low sofa, Humbly accepted his refreshments with a click of his tongue.

"I had no notion you could be such a tyrant."

Addy poured herself a cup of tea, although she ignored the various pastries.

"This was your idea, if you will recall," she reminded him.

"That was because I did not properly comprehend the Machiavellian delight that artists take in torturing their poor models. It is little wonder most people look stiff and unpleasantly grim in portraits."

She gave a chuckle at his ridiculous moanings. "I assure you I have been excessively kind, compared to most artists."

A distinct twinkle entered the sherry brown eyes as he took a large bite of a lemon tart.

"Perhaps our definitions of kind are different. To keep an old man away from his beloved tarts is in my estimation cruel in the extreme."

Addy settled back in the cushions, her frayed nerves slowly soothed by her companion's undemanding presence.

"I am so glad you have come for a visit."

"As am I, my dear." He offered her a sweet smile. "Tell me, did you enjoy the ball last evening?"

Her gaze abruptly dropped to the steam rising from her cup. There was little doubt that Mr. Humbly had sensed the brittle tension that filled the carriage on the drive home. Or the fact that Adam and Addy had not even glanced in one another's direction. Still, she felt distinctly uncomfortable discussing the stormy scene that had marred her evening.

"It was lovely to be among society again," she retorted vaguely. "What did you think of your first London ball?"

Humbly gave a surprising grimace. "Ah, well . . . I cannot say that I enjoyed being elbowed about or having my poor toes nearly crushed by a large woman in a hideous turban. But I did enjoy the monkey."

Addy widened her eyes at his words. "For shame, Mr. Humbly. That monkey sent several maidens screaming in terror."

He contentedly munched on his third lemon tart. "Yes,

it was the first moment all evening that the crowd had thinned enough to take in a breath.''

"It was a crush," she was forced to agree, recalling the numerous occasions her own toes had been trod upon and the oppressive heat.

"I am only happy that you had the opportunity to dance and meet with old acquaintances." Humbly tipped his head to one side, his expression faintly vague. "Was that not Lord Barclay you were speaking with?"

Addy's fingers tightened on her cup at the mention of the dashing Lord.

"Yes."

"Such a charming gentleman, if somewhat of a rogue. I recall he once stayed with your parents."

Addy was rather surprised that the Vicar even recalled the fleeting visit. Lord Barclay was a notorious snob and religiously avoided the neighboring village and those among the countryside he considered beneath him, which included all but her family and the Drakes.

"Yes, my mother wished to have him in one of her paintings."

"Quite understandable. He is very handsome."

Addy began to give a slow nod of her head, then with a faint sense of shock she realized that she did not care for the overly smooth features and pale blue eyes. There was no character upon his countenance, she acknowledged. Nothing but the shallow charm he used to his own advantage.

"I suppose," she said without any genuine enthusiasm.

Humbly did not seem to notice as he sipped his tea. "And quite taken with you, my dear."

Addy felt a flare of impatience. Dear heavens, she had spoken with Lord Barclay for less than ten minutes. Why did everyone assume that there had been more to the encounter than a brief greeting between distant acquaintances?

"He is a shocking flirt," she said in impatient tones. "He was merely amusing himself."

"Was he?" Humbly arched his brows in bland curiosity. "That was quite a bouquet of roses he sent this morning."

Addy flicked an indifferent glance toward the ludicrous number of vases filled with pale pink roses. She had known from the moment the extravagant bouquet had arrived it had not been intended as a tribute to her. No gentleman sent such a lavish gift to a proper lady.

Her first instinct had been to toss the lot of them out the back door. Only the knowledge that such a dramatic gesture was bound to create gossip among the servants had made her grit her teeth and allow them to be placed throughout the salon.

"He merely sent them to annoy Adam," she said with an edge of distaste. "For some reason the two of them detest one another."

"Do they?" Humbly took another hasty sip of his tea. "How very odd."

Odd?

More like annoying, ridiculous, and thoroughly without the least amount of sense, she told herself.

"Yes, it is," she said stoutly. "I suppose I shall never comprehend the workings of a gentleman's mind."

"I fear it is a rather tangled mess," the Vicar agreed in sympathy.

Swiftly realizing she had just insulted her guest, Addy widened her eyes with remorse.

"Oh, I was not referring to you, Mr. Humbly," she apologized. "You possess a very fine mind."

A hint of amusement glittered in the sherry eyes. "Thank you, my dear."

"If only all gentleman could be so rational and kindly tempered," she said with genuine longing. Heaven knew that her life would be considerably less nerve-wracking if Adam possessed this gentleman's sweet compassion.

"Ah well, I am old and well past the age when my pride is easily wounded and my heart cast into turmoil," he said gently. "A young gentleman is rarely rational when dealing with a maiden."

Her brows drew together. She did not believe for a moment that Adam's heart was in any way involved. But there was no doubting that he possessed more than his fair share of pride.

"It is all very maddening."

Humbly smiled with a gentle understanding. "Do not fear, Addy. All will be well." He leaned forward to regard the remaining tart. "Do you suppose I might have one more of those delicious tarts?"

Addy smiled ruefully. "Of course."

"Ah." Leaning back Humbly consumed the treat with obvious delight. "Your cook is a wonderful, wonderful woman."

Watching the old man's enjoyment, Addy did not hear the door softly open. Then a warning prickle raced over her skin making her head turn to discover Adam standing in the center of the room.

Although he was attired in a plain gray coat and gray striped waistcoat, there was nothing inconspicuous about his large male form. If anything the stark clothing only emphasized the chiseled strength of his broad chest and long legs. And, of course, there was nothing that could disguise the shimmering power of his mere presence. It was as much a part of him as the smoke gray eyes and hint of curl in the dark hair.

Just for a moment, their gazes met in silence. His probing, and hers wary, as they both attempted to gauge the other's temperament. Her breath seemed to catch as he took a step toward her then the spell was broken as Humbly abruptly noted his presence.

"Adam, welcome home."

With a faint shake of his head Adam turned from Addy and offered his guest a half bow.

"Thank you, Humbly. I trust Addy has kept you well entertained today?"

"Actually she has proven to be a dreadful taskmaster," the older man lightly teased. "I had no notion that completing a simple portrait could be so draining."

A faint smile touched Adam's lips. "It seems as if you are in need of a few hours reprieve. Perhaps you would care to join me at my club for dinner?"

Humbly obviously brightened at the notion. "Certainly. I should enjoy that very much."

"Good. I shall change and we will be on our way."

Barely aware that she was moving, Addy rose to her feet. She told herself that she was relieved Adam would not be spending the evening at home. Already she could feel her stomach tightening at having him in the same room. It would be a pleasure to enjoy a quiet dinner and perhaps read the new novel she had discovered at Hatchard's the previous week.

Yes, she should be delighted, so why did she feel that treacherous pang of disappointment?

"I should tell Cook you will not be here for dinner," she said with what she hoped was a passable smile. "Excuse me."

Not even glancing toward Adam, Addy turned to make her way through the still open door. She had taken several steps down the hall when she was halted by the sound of her name being called.

"Addy."

She paused for a full moment, before slowly turning to regard her husband. "Yes?"

"May I have a moment?"

She briefly considered a number of suitable excuses to escape.

She was feeling violently ill.

The kitchen was on fire.

Napoleon had landed.

But one glance into the steel gray of his eyes assured her that he would not be put off if the ceiling were tumbling about their heads.

"If you wish," she managed in even tones.

Moving forward he took her elbow and firmly steered her into the empty library. Once inside he closed the door and stepped away to regard her with a steady gaze.

"I owe you an apology," he at last said in abrupt tones.

It was not at all what Addy had been expecting and she discovered herself staring at him as if she were a half-wit.

"An apology?"

His lips twisted as he lifted one broad shoulder. "I did not intend to ruin your evening last night. My only excuse is that I have never cared for Lord Barclay."

Addy shifted her feet, not yet prepared to discuss their fiery confrontation.

"It hardly matters now."

"It does," he insisted, taking a step closer. "I wished you to have an evening that you could enjoy. At the time, however, I could only think of how many poor maidens that wretch has managed to embroil in scandal."

Had he simply apologized, Addy would have been happy to put the simmering anger to rest. She did not enjoy the prickling strain between them any more than Adam did. But once again he managed to flick her raw pride with his implication she was not to be trusted on her own.

"I am quite capable of avoiding scandal, regardless of what you believe."

The gray eyes flashed at the edge in her voice.

"I never believed that you would deliberately court scandal, Addy. But not even you can deny that Lord Barclay is precisely the sort of charming rascal who can turn the head of the most sensible lady."

She gave a disbelieving shake of her head. "I am a married lady."

The handsome features hardened. "Yes, but I am not so arrogant as to ignore the knowledge it was a marriage of necessity, not choice. You had no desire to wed me."

The sheer injustice of his words nearly stole her breath.

"You were hardly eager to take me as a bride," she retorted tartly.

A hint of impatience rippled over his countenance at her stubborn refusal to confess he had the right to question her loyalty.

"Which makes our situation all the more precarious. We must both make an effort at patience and understanding. It will take time to establish a relationship of complete trust."

Her chin tilted in defensive anger. "I am not the one who does not trust, Adam."

The male form stiffened as her sharp words rang through the vast room.

At last his lips curved into a humorless smile.

"Nor do you care, Addy." He offered her a bow. "Excuse me, I must change."

Addy watched in silence as he left the room, his back rigid and a dark cloud nearly visible about his large form.

Blast.

The last thing she had intended was to spark another argument. She had promised herself when she had left her chambers that morning, that she would ensure the calm, if somewhat icy atmosphere would be restored.

But somehow that calm seemed wretchedly elusive.

It was as if a protective wall between the two of them

had been tumbled away to expose all the emotions that they had battled to keep protected.

And for the life of her she did not know how to repair the damage.

Sprawled in a well-cushioned seat, Adam watched as Humbly eagerly studied the nearly empty room. After dining upon beef steak and discussing the latest politics with a few of his own cronies, Adam had deliberately steered the cheerful Vicar past the crowded card rooms to this small parlor at the back of the club. Although Humbly could reveal startling flashes of worldly wisdom he was still a country innocent that might very well be shocked by the rough talk and deep play of the town dandies.

Not seeming to mind their isolation from the other guests, Humbly sighed with obvious pleasure.

"How very pleasant this is."

"It is peaceful," Adam agreed. "At least on most occasions. There are always evenings when a few bucks over-indulge and create a scene. Or a dispute arises at the card tables."

Humbly gave a dismissive shrug. "Rather inevitable occurrences when a large number of gentleman are gathered together without the restraining influence of ladies. It reminds me somewhat of my schooldays."

Adam ruefully recalled his days at Oxford. "Thankfully without the ready beatings of the upperclassmen."

"True enough." Humbly chuckled.

With a ghostly silence a waiter appeared at Adam's side, bearing a silver tray that he set on a small table.

"Your brandy, sir."

"Thank you." Pouring two glasses of the fiery spirit he leaned forward to offer one to the Vicar. "Humbly."

Accepting his brandy, Humbly took a tentative sip and smiled in satisfaction.

"Ah, this is also a pleasant difference from schooldays," he murmured, settling back in his seat. "The brandy we would slip into our rooms was always of the most inferior quality."

Adam did not bother to hide his start of surprise. "Do not tell me you indulged in such shocking behavior?"

"I fear so." Humbly smiled nostalgically. "I was quite a rapscallion when I was young. More than once I was put to bed drunk as an emperor or lost my allowance in a card game. I was even sent down once for absconding with the headmaster's stash of cigars and sharing them with my friends."

Adam found it nearly impossible to believe the mild-mannered gentleman could ever have created such havoc. Even during the tumultuous years of youth.

"Good God, was your father furious?" he asked, shuddering at the mere thought of his own father's frigid disapproval.

"Actually he was surprisingly understanding," Humbly confessed. "He firmly believed that a gentleman should indulge his impulses when he was young. It did not take me long to tire of awakening with a thick head or rue the loss of my meager allowance. Being able to discover the truth for myself rather than being bullied into behaving had a far more lasting influence."

A vague sense of suspicion fluttered at the edge of Adam's mind.

Although Humbly rarely attempted to strong-arm his flock or badger them with prosy lectures, he did have a most subtle means of leading them down the path he desired. And he usually managed to do so without the victim ever suspecting that they were not making their own decisions every step of the way.

"I suppose that is true enough," he cautiously agreed.

"And, of course, I only had to be kicked in the head by our mule once to learn not to stand behind the beast," Humbly continued in a wry tone.

Adam abruptly took a large gulp of brandy. The reference to a mule abruptly reminded him of his stubborn wife. Hardly flattering he had to admit, but at the moment he was in no mood to be charitable.

Did the ungrateful woman have no notion how difficult it had been to seek her out and apologize? It had taken him the entire day to thrust aside his pride and convince himself that peace with his wife was worth any price.

And what had she done to thank him for his efforts?

She had tossed his apology back into his face and bristled with an outrage that was incomprehensible.

Of course, he was beginning to believe everything about Addy was incomprehensible.

His hand tightened upon his glass, but even as the surge of self-righteous anger raced through him, a tiny voice whispered in the back of his mind that Addy was not entirely to blame.

There would have been no need to apologize if he had not lost his head like a buffoon. He prided himself on his calm logic, but there had been nothing calm or logical about his reaction to seeing Lord Barclay hovering over his wife.

Rather than waiting to deliver his warning to Addy in the privacy of their own home, he had flown across the room like a demented husband and created precisely the sort of antagonism within Addy he had been most determined to avoid.

He heaved a faint sigh. "I wish I were so swift to learn from my mistakes," he muttered.

"Do you speak of Addy?" the Vicar demanded with surprising perception.

Adam sighed again. "Yes, I fear I made a hash of last

evening. I intended to provide her with an opportunity to laugh and mingle with others. Instead I merely pushed her further away.''

"She did not wish to be warned from Lord Barclay?''

Adam's lips thinned at Addy's stormy reaction. "No. Indeed, she was deeply offended at the thought I did not trust her.''

"And do you trust her?'' Humbly demanded in soft tones.

Adam felt a restless impatience rush through him.

He was not a villain.

He was simply wise enough to regard his marriage without ridiculous expectations.

"I think the notion of a flirtation with a handsome and charming rake would be a temptation for any lady. Especially one who finds her own husband tediously dull.''

"Perhaps she needs to be kicked in the head by a mule.''

Adam blinked in surprise at the absurd suggestion.

He might desire to shake some sense into her, but not even he would desire her to be kicked in her lovely head.

"What did you say?''

Humbly appeared a bit sheepish. "Well, we were discussing an effective means of learning a much needed lesson.''

"I do not believe Addy often stands behind mules, although she is as stubborn as one,'' Adam retorted dryly.

"I was thinking more in terms of discovering the truth about rakes.''

Adam once again felt a prickle of suspicion that he was being nudged in a direction he did not wish to take.

"And what truth is that?''

Humbly smiled with sweet innocence. "That they are all very well to dance the waltz with, or to take along on a drive through the park, but they are notoriously unfaithful and overly inclined to indulge their own pleasure.''

"Obviously. That is why they are considered rakes.''

"I believe Addy has forgotten just how uncomfortable it is to have a rake about. Perhaps you should remind her."

Adam's brows snapped together. "You are surely not suggesting I encourage a connection between my wife and Lord Barclay?"

"Goodness, no."

"Good." Adam's countenance hardened. "Because I would put a bullet through the scoundrel before I would allow him close to Addy."

The Vicar's lips seemed to twitch at his fierce words, but his expression remained unchanged.

"No. I am suggesting that *you* become the rake."

"A rake? Me?" Adam recoiled in disbelief. "You must be mad."

"Well, I suppose there are those who would agree with that," Humbly said wryly. "But I am merely attempting to consider the simplest solution to your troubles. You fear that Addy finds you dull and might be tempted by a rake, so why not reveal just how unpleasant life could be if you were indeed less honorable and dependable?"

Adam wondered if the Vicar was sipping his brandy a bit too swiftly.

"It is absurd."

"So is chastising your wife in the midst of a ball," Humbly retorted pointedly.

The thrust slid directly home and Adam briefly closed his eyes as he accepted the pang of guilt.

He could not deny that his own methods of dealing with Addy had been a spectacular failure. On every occasion he had managed to do precisely the wrong thing.

Could it be any worse to follow Humbly's ludicrous suggestion?

Could he indeed reveal to Addy that there were more terrible fates than possessing a husband who was loyal and faithful?

He gave a sharp shake of his head. "Gads, I do not know."

"At least give it some thought," Humbly said gently.

Adam smiled without humor. "Well one thing is certain, I could not create a greater muddle than I have already."

Humbly gave a sudden chuckle. "And who knows, you might decide there is something to be said for indulging in a bit of nonsense now and then."

Adam grimaced, not at all certain he wasn't the one who was mad.

"We shall see."

Chapter Five

The night might have come straight from a Gothic novel.

Lightning slashed the midnight sky, followed closely by crashing thunder that rattled the windows and made Addy's teeth clench in unease. Even the wind howled with a mighty force, slashing the rain against the townhouse and making the shutters bang in an ominous fashion.

Huddled beside the blazing fire, Addy pulled her robe closer about her body.

She had gone to bed long ago, after a lonely dinner and hours spent staring at the same page of her novel. She had been determined not to be discovered by Adam and Mr. Humbly awaiting their return like a pathetic waif.

It had been no good, however.

After tossing and turning for hours as she strained to hear the sound of Adam's carriage, Addy had at last risen from her bed and made her way downstairs. With such a storm raging outside no one would find it odd that she was too nervous to sleep.

Glancing toward the delicate Louis XIV clock on the mantel Addy clenched her hands in her lap.

Two o'clock.

Where the blazes was Adam?

He never visited his club without returning punctually at midnight. It was, in fact, a source of irritation to her at the manner in which he could always be depended upon to step through the door just as the clock would strike the hour. Never a minute early, never a minute late.

It was unnatural.

But this evening she realized that it was far more irritating not to have the slightest notion where Adam was. Or even what he might be doing.

Surely he realized that she would be concerned at such uncharacteristic behavior?

A soft knock on the door followed by the familiar form of the housekeeper had Addy hastily smoothing her expression to a calm indifference. She would not allow anyone to realize she was riddled with unease.

"Would you care for more tea, Mrs. Drake?" the older woman demanded.

Addy glanced toward the pot of tea that had long ago grown cold. "Thank you, no."

The room was abruptly lit by a jagged flash of lightning. With a click of her tongue the housekeeper moved to pull the curtains closed.

"A nasty night. Far too nasty to be out."

Addy smiled wryly, realizing she was not the only one being kept from her sleep by Adam's absence.

"Why do you not go to bed, Mrs. Hall? Chatson will see to Mr. Drake and Mr. Humbly when they return."

"I can not think what is keeping them," Mrs. Hall burst out. "Mr. Drake is always home by midnight."

Addy forced a stiff smile to her lips. "No doubt he and

his guest are enjoying themselves and have simply lost track of time.''

The housekeeper gave a loud sniff at the offhand explanation. ''I have never known Mr. Drake to lose track of time. He is very particular about that sort of thing.''

Obsessive more like, Addy inwardly corrected.

''Yes.''

''I fear that they may have been set upon by footpads. Or suffered an accident in this foul weather.''

They were fears that had run through Addy's own mind more than once. London could be a dangerous place at night with any number of criminals willing to attack a lone coach. And of course, the weather was indeed ghastly enough to have caused an accident.

But then common sense had intruded.

If something had occurred at least one of the grooms would surely return to the house and inform her. Or even a passerby.

''I am certain they are fine, Mrs. Hall,'' she said in tones that held more confidence than she felt. ''Go to bed and I promise I will call if I hear anything.''

''It's queer if you ask me,'' the older woman grumbled, as she made her way to the door. ''Very queer.''

Waiting until Mrs. Hall had left the room, Addy gave a shake of her head and returned her gaze to the dancing flames.

She should follow her own advice and simply go to bed, she chastised herself. She was certainly accomplishing nothing by sitting in this chair and brooding like some overanxious wife.

It was absurd.

Oddly, however, she could not seem to summon energy to make the push to rise from the chair and return to her room. Instead she remained curled in the chair, drifting toward a light doze.

It was nearly half an hour later when the sound of a male voice loudly singing a naughty ditty startled her awake.

Rising from her chair Addy attempted to clear her foggy mind. Not an easy task when it seemed that some strange man had intruded into her home and was determined to rouse the entire household with his scandalous song.

Debating whether to hide or make the attempt to scurry to her chambers and lock the door, Addy was startled nearly out of her skin when the door to the library crashed open and a large male form staggered into the room.

A scream rose to her lips, but before it could shatter the sudden silence, Addy froze in disbelief.

The intruder was Adam.

Or at least it appeared to be Adam.

With a wide gaze she studied the dark hair that was astonishingly ruffled and cravat that had been pulled loose to hang about his neck. Even more shocking, a wide grin split his countenance, giving him an air of boyish devilment.

Stepping forward Addy gave a slow shake of her head. "Adam?"

It seemed to take a moment for his gaze to focus upon her slender form.

"Addy? What the devil are you doing up?"

Although his words were deliberately concise, Addy did not miss the faint slur.

"I was concerned when you did not come home," she said with a frown.

"But I did come home. Unless I have managed to stumble into the wrong address." He glanced briefly about the book-lined room. "No, this looks very much like my library."

Wondering if he had taken a damaging blow to the head, Addy regarded him warily.

"It is very late."

"Is it?"

"Yes." She paused for a moment. "Do you feel well?"

His grin abruptly widened. "Never better. It is a lovely evening, is it not?"

Addy was struck by a new suspicion at his peculiar, giddy manner.

"Have you been drinking?"

His brow furrowed as if it were a difficult task to ponder her question.

"I believe I did have a little brandy at the club," he at last confessed. "Very fine brandy, if I recall."

"I would say that it was more than a little."

"Perhaps."

Not at all certain how to react to the unexpected sight of Adam cast to the wind, Addy cleared her throat.

"Is something troubling you, Adam?"

He blinked in befuddled surprise. "What would make you ask?"

"I have never known you to become bosky. Indeed, you have always claimed that a true gentleman keeps his wits about him at all times."

"I am not bosky," he denied, only to ruin his claim when he gave a loud hiccup. "Just a trifle foxed. Besides, you were the one to bemoan my rigid refusal to indulge myself in the vast array of entertainments that London offers. I am simply following your advice."

Addy stiffened at his accusation. "I see."

"Now, I came in here for something . . . ah, brandy."

His gaze swept across the room as if unable to recall where the sideboard was located and Addy's frown deepened.

"Are you sure you are in need of more?"

He lifted one broad shoulder. "Why not?"

"You seem to have had quite enough."

His smile became mocking as he returned his gaze to her troubled countenance.

"I thought you admired gentlemen of excess, Addy."

She ignored his barb and attempted to stir a measure of his usually indomitable common sense.

"You are going to be very ill tomorrow."

"That is tomorrow. Tonight I desire more brandy."

He took a step forward only to sway in an alarming fashion. With a swift motion Addy rushed toward him, managing to keep him upright by placing both hands upon his chest.

"Careful."

"I believe the floor is moving," he said in surprised tones, gazing down at her upturned face. "Rather peculiar, do you not think?"

"You really should go to bed, Adam," she pleaded softly.

A silence descended as the gray eyes darkened to smoke. A new, tingling electricity filled the air.

"I do not suppose you intend to join me there?"

Addy's breath caught in her throat as she realized just how close she was to the large, harshly male form.

"Adam."

His lips twisted as he reached out to fold his arms about her waist. With a small jerk he had molded her firmly against him.

"Is it shocking that I should desire my wife at my side?"

A flare of panic raced through Addy at the smoldering heat she could sense in his taut body.

Always before, Adam had kept his passions sternly controlled. When he came to her it was with a cool control that made her feel his presence was more necessity than pleasure.

Tonight, however, there was nothing cool or controlled about the hands that were beginning to run a restless path over the curve of her back and down to her hips. A sharp shiver raced through her as her heart began to pound at a hectic pace.

"You do not know what you are saying."

"Ah, I know all too well," he muttered, lowering his

head to rub his cheek against her own. A bolt of heat shot through Addy as the stubble of his beard rasped over her soft skin and his breath teased her ear. "Do you know that you always smell of lilacs?"

Dazed by the jumbled sensations that wracked her body Addy could barely concentrate upon his husky words. Dear heavens, she had never realized how disturbing the touch of his strong male hands could be. Or noticed how the scent of his warm skin could send a tingle down her spine.

"It is from the soap I use," she ridiculously muttered.

"Mmm ... I like it," he whispered, moving to lightly nip the lobe of her ear. At the same moment his hands lifted to begin removing the pins from her hair in an impatient fashion.

Wondering how she could feel as if she were drowning when she was standing in the center of the library, Addy clutched at the lapels of his coat. Something seemed to be stirring deep within her. Something that was a mixture of pleasure, excitement, and a building need.

She closed her eyes as his seeking lips moved from her ear to the tender arch of her neck.

"What are you doing?" she demanded in a choked voice.

"I wish to see your hair about your shoulders." His fingers plunged into the heavy curls now freed from their tidy bun. "Such beautiful hair. Gypsy hair."

Giving a faint tug on her curls he arched her head backward to offer him greater access to her throat. The world halted as his lips stroked the frantic pulse just above her collarbone.

Adam gave a faint groan of satisfaction as she instinctively curved closer to the searing heat of his body.

"Adam," she whispered, struggling desperately to summon a shred of sense among the spiraling sensations.

"Yes?" he murmured, nibbling his way over her collarbone and down to the curve of her breast.

Addy's knees nearly buckled, scandalous images of being laid upon the carpet and allowing his large form to cover her flickering through her mind.

How would it feel to have those restless fingers stroking her bare skin? Or to feel the hungry lips caressing her with a building urgency that would stoke the flames smoldering within her to a white-hot fire?

With her breath coming in soft pants she made a last bid for sanity.

"Do you wish me to call for your valet?"

"Gads, no!" Abruptly he lifted his head to gaze down at her with a fierce need. The eyes she had once thought impossibly cold now glittered with a searing heat. "What I wish is to have you kiss me."

"Adam, I am not sure . . ."

"Just one kiss, Addy," he pleaded in husky tones. "One kiss that has nothing to do with duty or wifely obligation. One kiss that you give freely."

She should say no.

Not only was Adam clearly not in his right mind, but she was obviously consumed with some sort of fever. What other explanation could there be for the flood of shivering pleasure that was turning her bones to melted butter?

But even as the voice of caution whispered in the back of her mind, her lips were parting in silent invitation.

Tonight, for whatever reason, she wanted his kisses. No, needed his kisses, she acknowledged as her stomach knotted with a sharp ache of desire.

Closely watching her features soften with capitulation Adam gave a rumbling sound deep in his throat. Then moving his hands to gently frame her face, he captured her lips in an ardent, seeking kiss.

Accustomed to discreet, deliberate kisses Addy was unprepared for the reckless yearning in his demanding pressure.

Her head spun as he plundered the softness of her mouth, murmuring words of encouragement as her lips parted further to allow him access to the moist temptation within.

Addy was lost in a dazzling world of building desire. She did not care if Adam were in his right mind or not. She simply wished to be swept along the torrential currents that promised sweet satisfaction.

She felt Adam's hands abruptly drop to her shoulders. Then lifting his head he regarded her with dazed eyes.

Bewildered at the sudden halt to his bewitching caresses Addy regarded him in confusion. He seemed as if he desired to speak, but even as his mouth opened he slowly swayed sideways. He groaned, then before she could even move he had toppled to the carpet.

With wide eyes Addy regarded her husband lying sound asleep at her feet.

Someone was pounding upon his head.

Adam groaned and tried to shift from the merciless demon. It did no good, however. The pounding continued and now a red-hot pain had been jolted to life behind his eyes. He groaned again, slowly becoming aware that the pounding was not actually in his head, but rather coming from the closed door.

He also became aware that he was lying upon his bed without a stitch of clothing beneath the light blanket.

He lifted a weak hand to press against his throbbing head.

The devil take that wretched vicar, he silently seethed. As soon as he was capable of dragging himself from his bed he was going to throttle the devious man.

Unable to bear any more pounding, Adam at last wrenched open his heavy eyes and glared at the door.

"Good God, Dobson, stop that infernal banging," he commanded in exasperation.

The pounding blessedly ceased, but as the door swung open Adam realized that it was not his valet intruding into his much needed rest, but his wife.

"Good morning, Adam," she said softly, moving forward with a glass of some brownish liquid in her hand.

His breath caught as he watched her graceful movement and the manner in which her raven curls shimmered in the late morning sunlight.

Suddenly the memories of the night before crashed through his aching mind.

He remembered returning home and discovering Addy in the library. He remembered the smell of sweet lilacs. The feel of her satin hair. The taste of her lips. The feel of her trembling with desire in his arms.

Desire.

And then all had gone black.

A sharp, startling flare of disappointment raced through him.

For the first time in all the months that they had been married Addy had not grown rigid at his touch.

Instead she had been warm and inviting and as deliciously passionate as he could possibly desire.

Heaven had been in his grasp and he had ruined it by tumbling onto his face like a common greenhorn.

His hands clenched in frustration before the sharp pang in his head forced him to relax his coiled muscles.

Very well. He had failed to take advantage of his opportunity last evening, but that did not mean there would be no further chances.

He could make Addy desire him.

He could not give up hope.

Feeling his body stir at the mere memory of her heated kisses, Adam carefully shifted the blanket as she came to a halt beside the bed.

"How do you feel?" she demanded.

"Ghastly."

"I feared you might." She held out the glass. "I brought you something that will help."

Pushing himself to a seated position he took the offered glass and cautiously sniffed the strange mixture.

"What is it?"

"My own recipe. I use to make it for my father."

Knowing how often Lord Morrow must have woken with a thick head, Adam readily lifted the glass and drained the contents down his dry throat.

"Dear heavens," he gasped, shuddering as the awful stuff hit his stomach. "You could have warned me."

Her expression remained composed, but there was a noticeable hint of amusement in the dark eyes.

Evil wench.

"It is not so bad."

"It is horrid. What did you put in there?"

"Nothing more than a few harmless herbs."

"Weeds, more likely," he grumbled.

She arched a raven brow. "I did not force you to drink yourself senseless."

He once again imagined his hands about the Vicar's plump neck.

"No, I can safely lay that upon Humbly's doorstep."

"Are you saying that a vicar encouraged you to become drunk?"

Abruptly realizing they were treading upon dangerous ground he shifted to place the empty glass upon a side table. Not only could he not explain Humbly's ridiculous notion to play the role of the rake, but he was also wise enough to realize that Addy was bound to be skittish about her fervent response to his kisses.

He could sense her unease in the manner she so rigidly avoided glancing at his bare chest and the determined distance she kept from his wide bed.

He did not want to blunder and send her scurrying back behind her icy barriers.

Not when he was so close.

"To be honest I recall very little of what occurred last night," he said in an offhand tone. "One minute Humbly and I were finishing our meal at the club and the next I was awakening with the feeling I had gone several losing rounds with Gentleman Jackson."

The faintest hint of color touched her cheeks. "You do not recall coming home?"

"No. Why do you ask?"

"It is nothing," she assured him hastily.

"I hope I did not wake you?"

"No, I was still up."

He forced a hint of surprise to his countenance. "It must have been very late."

"Yes."

"You could not sleep?" he found himself probing. He couldn't deny a bit of curiosity as to why she had been in the library at such an hour.

"I was concerned when you did not return," she reluctantly confessed. "Mrs. Hall was convinced you had been overtaken by footpads."

Adam felt an odd twinge in the region of his heart.

She had been concerned?

About him?

Amazing.

"Forgive me," he said softly. "It did not occur to me that you would be worried."

She stiffened slightly, as if she realized that she had given more away than she had intended.

"I am your wife. Of course I was concerned."

He smiled wryly. "Yes."

Their gazes tangled for a silent moment, as if each were testing the subtle but undeniable shift in their relationship.

Then without warning their privacy was interrupted as Humbly surged into the room with a bright smile.

"Good morning. Forgive me for intruding, but I wished to see how Adam was this morning."

Adam flashed the Vicar a sour glance. "I feel as if I have been kicked in the head," he retorted in pointed tones.

The devilish man merely chuckled at his words.

"Ah well, it was a rousing good time."

"I must trust your word as to that," he muttered.

"I had no notion you could sing so well, my son."

Adam winced at the foggy memory of leading the entire club in several off-key songs.

"Adam was singing?" Addy demanded in surprise.

"Yes, indeed, although his choice in songs was rather naughty," Humbly teased.

Adam's gaze narrowed. He was supposed to be playing the role of a rake, not a buffoon.

"I do not believe Addy is interested in the details of our evening, Humbly."

"Ah. Quite right. Not at all the thing for female ears."

Addy stabbed him with a curious gaze. "I did not know you could sing."

"It is not a talent I indulge in often," he assured her.

Clearly having enjoyed the brief ribbing, Humbly gave a faint nod of his head.

"Well, I shall leave you to recover from your heavy head. Do not forget you promised Mr. Bates that we would attend his wife's soiree tonight."

"Gads." Adam sighed as the older gentleman slipped from the room.

He had nearly forgotten his encounter with Bates as he was stumbling from the club.

"Mr. Bates?" Addy demanded with a faint frown.

"An old school chum of mine. I believe I did tell him

that we would make an appearance. I thought you would be pleased.''

"Yes, of course," she murmured, although she did not appear delighted by the notion.

Adam shifted uncomfortably. His head still ached, his stomach rolled with an unpleasant queasiness and he desperately desired to clean his teeth.

More than anything he was in dire need of a chamber pot.

"If you do not mind, my dear, I believe I shall take a hot bath. Perhaps that will clear my foggy thoughts."

Addy gave a ready nod, although her faintly troubled expression lingered. It was evident his unusual behavior was keeping her off guard.

A promising sign, he tried to reassure himself.

"I shall call for Dobson."

With swift steps she had left the room, leaving behind the scent of lilacs in the air. Adam breathed in the sweet aroma. He hoped it was only the first of countless occasions when the tantalizing scent filled his chamber.

Chapter Six

The warm hands ran a restless path down her back, stroking her shivering skin, and sending a liquid fire through her veins. Addy arched closer to the delicious male form as hungry lips crushed her mouth.

She was being consumed, but she did not care. Nothing mattered but that soon she would be released from the fierce ache that haunted her . . .

Soon.

"Addy. Are you finished? Addy?"

With an abrupt jerk, Addy was wrenched from her delectable daydream. She gave a dazed blink to discover herself seated in the salon holding a forgotten drawing pad in her hand.

A flustered heat stung her cheeks as she realized that the Vicar was regarding her with a searching gaze.

Dear heavens, what was the matter with her? she wondered with a flare of panic. A lady did not sit in a salon with a respectable vicar and think of such things.

Indeed, a lady did not think of such things at all.

But no matter how many times she chastised herself for her traitorous thoughts, Addy simply could not dismiss the memories of the night before.

Why had Adam never touched her with such passion before? Why had he not kissed her as if he were desperate for the mere taste of her? Why had he not swept aside her reserve and demanded her response?

She gave a faint shake of her head at the futile longings.

Now was certainly not the moment to brood upon Adam's strange behavior. Not with Mr. Humbly regarding her with obvious curiosity.

"I am sorry. What did you say?"

The older man's lips twitched as if he found something amusing in her distraction.

"I inquired if we were finished for the day."

"Oh, yes. Forgive me."

Settling back in a more comfortable position, Humbly watched as she set aside her drawing pad.

"I do not mean to intrude, my dear, but it does not seem as if your mind is upon your work today."

"I suppose I am rather distracted," she conceded reluctantly, knowing that she could hardly deny the obvious.

"Is there anything I can help you with?"

Addy paused. She could hardly confess what was upon her mind, but perhaps the Vicar could ease the growing concern that had begun to plague her lately.

"It is no doubt ridiculous, but I can not help but be worried about Adam."

"Oh? Is he still nursing a thick head?"

She waved a dismissive hand. Her father had nursed a countless number of thick heads with no ill effects.

"I do not refer to his head, which no doubt will heal with time."

The gray brows rose. "Then what is troubling you?"

"It is very unlike him to overindulge in brandy."

Surprisingly Mr. Humbly merely smiled at her concern. "Ah well, every gentleman can be forgiven for an occasional lapse."

Every gentleman except Adam, she silently acknowledged. He did not have lapses of any sort. Never.

"He did not seem angry or disturbed?"

"Not at all," the Vicar denied in firm tones. "He was in the finest spirits. I assure you it did my heart good to see him ease his guard and simply enjoy himself."

"Yes, I suppose," she retorted in dubious tones.

Humbly widened his eyes. "My dear, I thought you would be pleased."

"Pleased?"

"Well, you did complain he was far too rigid. You even wished that he would be more like your father."

Addy shifted uneasily. Certainly she wished that Adam would not be so uncompromisingly proper. And that he would occasionally lower his guard enough to enjoy a bit of frivolity. But had she actually claimed that she wished him to be another Lord Morrow?

"I suppose," she reluctantly agreed.

Humbly gave a sudden chuckle. "Do you recall when your father had been drinking at the local inn and he became lost on his way home and he spent the entire night in my rose bushes? Or the time he accepted the wager to hold up the mail coach and he was forced to hide from the magistrate for a fortnight? Ah yes, Lord Morrow is certainly a gentleman who knows how to drink freely from the cup of life."

Addy attempted to hide her wince at the unpleasant memories. For the past few weeks she had felt a nostalgic ache to return home and be among her joyous, unpredictable family. Humbly's words, however, were an unwelcome reminder that the Morrow household was not without a few trials.

"He does know how to enjoy himself," she retorted in low tones.

Seemingly unaware of her discomfort the Vicar smiled brightly. "As does your mother. Such a beautiful, spirited woman. She has never been bound by the stuffy rules of society."

Addy's own smile was wan. Her mother was beyond spirited, she ruefully acknowledged. She was reckless, impulsive and wholly enchanted with gentlemen young enough to be her own sons.

"No, she does not concern herself with rules."

"So you see, I thought you would be happy to think that Adam is willing to put aside his conventional manner upon occasion."

Addy gave a restless shake of her head. The older man was beginning to tangle her thoughts.

"I just do not comprehend why he would do so now," she complained.

"Who can say?" With a valiant struggle, the Vicar rose to his feet. "If you will excuse me, I believe I shall have a brief rest before dinner."

"Of course."

Addy watched her guest slowly make his way from the room. If she had hoped that Mr. Humbly would ease her concern, she had been sorely mistaken, she sighed.

It was ridiculous to presume that Adam was somehow attempting to please her. He was not the sort of gentleman to alter his lifestyle to please anyone.

There had to be something else disturbing him.

But what?

She was no closer to an answer when the housekeeper bustled into the room and plucked the empty tea tray from the table.

"I see the Vicar enjoyed his lemon tarts," Mrs. Hall said with a sniff.

Addy smiled wryly at the memory of Humbly gobbling the tarts with open relish.

"Yes, he does possess a fondness for them."

Surprisingly the servant's countenance remained set in lines of disapproval.

"May I ask how long Mr. Humbly will be staying?"

"I am uncertain," Addy admitted with a frown. "Does it matter?"

"For a man of God he has not been a good influence upon this household," Mrs. Hall readily spoke her mind. "First by encouraging Mr. Drake to remain out all hours of the night, and now dragging him to the Bates's soiree."

Addy regarded the servant with a curious gaze. "Is there something wrong with Mr. Bates?"

"Not him. A very decent gentleman who has been a friend to Mr. Drake for years. I am referring to his sister."

"His sister?"

Mrs. Hall gave a click of her tongue. "Not that it is my place to speak ill of my betters, but she has always made a pest of herself when Mr. Drake is in London. Sending him notes, following him about town, and even attempting to compromise him into marriage. At last Mr. Drake was forced to stop attending any function she might be at."

Addy could not disguise her shock.

"Good heavens."

"And she wasn't the only maiden to make a fool of herself over Mr. Drake," the housekeeper continued in a warning voice. "He has always been a great favorite among the fairer sex."

Adam?

Adam was a great favorite among women?

He had been pursued and nearly compromised?

"Oh," she at last murmured.

Mrs. Hall wagged a finger of doom. "I would suggest

that you keep a close eye on that Miss Bates. She is a vixen, make no mistake.''

Having heard quite enough, Addy firmly cleared her throat. For some reason the thought of Adam being pursued by determined young maidens left a sour taste in her mouth.

''That will be all, Mrs. Hall.''

Adam was a man of purpose.

After gathering all the pertinent facts and careful consideration he chose his course of action and moved forward with confident assurance.

It was the only means of accomplishing a goal, he had always told himself. To hesitate or endlessly debate a decision left one floundering in incompetency.

Tonight, however, he discovered himself pausing several long moments before at last pushing open the connecting door to Addy's room.

It was not that he was nervous, he was swift to reassure himself. It was merely a matter of caution. Unlike himself, Addy was a woman very much prey to her emotions, although she sternly attempted to pretend a cool demeanor. It made it difficult to predict how she would react at any given moment.

A rather unnerving realization for a gentleman of logic.

Moving further into the room Adam caught sight of Addy seated at her dressing table.

In the glow of the candlelight she appeared breathtakingly lovely. The pale rose of her satin gown skimmed the lush curves and gave a tantalizing glimpse of the swell of her bosom. The raven curls had been loosened into ringlets atop her head with a few wispy strands brushing her ivory cheeks.

A stunning, nearly overwhelming surge of desire slammed into him at the sight of her elegant form.

He vividly remembered how she felt, trembling in his

arms. The satin of her skin. The sound of her rasping breath filling the air.

It would be so easy to pluck her from the chair and take the few steps to her wide bed. His entire body ached to do so.

But the realization he had no notion if she would melt with warmth or stiffen with resignation made him savagely stifle his instinctive impulse.

Patience, he sternly cautioned himself.

Only time would tell if he and Addy could overcome the barriers between them. To rush her now would surely spell disaster.

Once again in control of himself, Adam firmly crossed the delicate floral carpet to halt at her side.

"Good evening, Addy."

Intent on choosing the proper pair of gloves, Addy gave a small jump of surprise as she glanced upward.

"Adam."

His gaze drifted over her pale countenance. In the flickering light her skin glowed with the rich luster of pearls while her eyes darkened to mysterious pools of ebony. He halted as he reached the tempting softness of her lips.

"You look lovely."

As if sensing his restless passion she dropped her heavy lashes over her eyes in a flustered manner.

"Thank you. Is there something you need?"

He stifled his instinctive groan.

He knew precisely what he needed. Unfortunately he was not certain she needed, nor desired the same thing.

"Not at all," he forced himself to lie.

"I am not late, am I?"

"No, I am early."

"Oh."

Taking a deep breath Adam forced himself to plunge into his reason for intruding into her chamber.

"It occurred to me that I have been very remiss," he said, his clipped tones covering his vague embarrassment.

Her gaze flew upward in surprise.

"Remiss?"

"I should have realized that every woman enjoys wearing a bauble or two. Especially when they are mingling with society."

Pressing the box he had brought with him into her hands, he watched as she slowly lifted the lid to reveal the delicate diamond necklace and matching earrings. A smile curved his lips as she gasped in delight.

He had chosen well.

"Adam," she breathed.

"Do you like them?"

"They are lovely." She lifted a puzzled gaze. "But it is too much."

"Nonsense," he denied. "Of course if there is something else you prefer we could always exchange them."

"No. They are perfect."

He rewarded her with a warm smile. "Good. May I help you?" He reached down to pluck the earrings from the box and attached them to her earlobes. Then with great care he draped the necklace about her throat and clasped the tiny lock. Of their own volition his fingers stroked the fiery diamonds that lay on her pale skin. "They look very good on you."

Her breath caught as she met his shimmering gaze. "I do not know what to say."

"There is nothing you need say. I only want you to enjoy them." Unable to resist, Adam bent slowly downward to lightly brush her mouth with his own. Her lips parted in silent invitation, but he pulled sharply back. He did not trust his precarious control. Not with that damnable bed looming so tantalizingly near. "I shall see you downstairs."

Not daring to linger to hear her response Adam turned

and swiftly made his way out of her chamber. Even when he reached the hallway he kept his reluctant feet moving toward the staircase and down to the front salon.

For a gentleman of unshakable control he was suddenly finding it absurdly difficult to keep his hands off his own wife.

Entering the room it was a relief to discover Humbly already settled upon a sofa. He was in desperate need of a distraction from his fantasies.

"Good evening, Humbly," he murmured, moving to lean against the mantel.

"Ah, Adam. You are feeling better I trust?"

"I am recovering." He glanced pointedly at the glass of brandy in his guest's hand. "You will understand, however, if I do not join you in a drink?"

"Certainly." The Vicar regarded him with a steady gaze. "I do hope that you have not given up on our notion, Adam?"

Adam briefly closed his eyes as he recalled the humiliating end to his evening. Bad enough to have entertained half of London with his bawdy songs, to collapse at the feet of his wife was outside enough.

"Gads, Humbly, I have accomplished nothing more than to make a fool of myself with your ridiculous notion."

Humbly abruptly leaned forward. "On the contrary. Addy is very disturbed by your night of revelry. She questioned me quite sharply on what could be disturbing you. It is obvious she is beginning to question her desire for a more exciting marriage."

Adam grimaced. "It still seems absurd."

"You must give it time," Humbly chided. "As the good book says, 'Be strong and let your heart take courage.' "

"I would take far more courage if I did not feel like a lobcock," he said dryly.

"You do wish to improve your relationship with your wife, do you not?"

Adam felt a flare of impatience. "Of course I do."

There was a small silence as the Vicar studied him with a discomforting intensity.

"Tell me, Adam, just what is it that you do desire from Addy?"

Adam frowned at the unexpected question. "I wish to see her more content in our marriage."

"Nothing else?" Humbly prodded.

"What do you mean?"

"Do you desire love?"

Adam abruptly straightened. Love? What did that have to do with marriage? Respect, honor, and loyalty were the ingredients for a satisfying relationship. Love was for those silly enough to be a victim of their unpredictable emotions.

"We did not wed for love," he said stiffly.

"That does not make us not long for it in our lives. Did you know that I was once engaged?"

Adam blinked at the mere thought of Humbly with a maiden. Surely he was a born bachelor?

"No."

"Sally Falton." Humbly heaved a reminiscent sigh. "A bewitching maiden who was as sweet as she was beautiful. I met her the year before I traveled to Surrey. Ah, what a lovely summer we had."

"Why did you not wed?"

"Her father was ambitious and not about to allow his daughter to throw herself away upon a lowly vicar." Humbly shrugged. "Like Addy, poor Sally was expected to save the family from financial ruin."

Adam felt a sharp pang. He did not like to recall that Addy had been forced into marriage.

"A bad break," he murmured.

"Yes. At the time I thought I should never recover from my disappointment."

Adam tried and failed to imagine this gentleman pining with unrequited love.

"Obviously you did recover."

"Not until far too late, I fear," he mourned.

"What?"

"At the time I considered myself a martyr on the altar of love." Humbly dropped his gaze to study the brandy in his glass. "Sally was my true partner and if I could not have her then I would live a life of tragic solitude. When one is young everything is very dramatic and excessively uncompromising."

Adam studied his guest with growing curiosity. He sensed that Humbly had a very specific point to his seemingly random reminiscences.

"I suppose that is true enough."

"The years passed and while I learned that Sally had wed and was happily producing a brood of children, I still clung to my bittersweet memories. I swore that my heart would never be touched again."

Adam's curiosity deepened to suspicion. What was the wily old fox up to now?

"I am sorry."

"So am I." Humbly slowly raised his gaze, his expression unnaturally somber. "I was a fool. Rather than allowing Sally to become a sweet memory I continued to cling to my disappointment. I failed to realize that there were beautiful, wonderful women all about me. The next thing I knew I was an old man all alone."

Adam lifted a dark brow, thinking on the endless guests that crowded into the Vicarage.

"You are hardly alone, Humbly."

The Vicar allowed a whimsical smile to touch his lips. "Certainly I have many friends whom I hold dear to my heart. But there is nothing that can replace the love of a wife and children to fill your house. Had I not been so stubborn I would have sought a love that was possible rather than long for the unobtainable. There is nothing romantic about turning your back on the promise of happiness directly before you.''

Abruptly realizing what the old fool was suggesting Adam gave a sharp shake of his head.

It was ludicrous.

''I assure you, Humbly, that Addy will never offer her heart, even if I were to desire it.''

Humbly waved a pudgy hand. ''You are bound together. Would the years not pass more pleasantly with affection between the two of you?''

Adam battled back the vivid images that threatened to rise to mind. Images of Addy's countenance lighting with happiness when he entered the room. The two of them seated by the fire discussing their day. Addy in his bed with her arms open.

Such thoughts could only lead to disappointment. And in the end, bitterness.

Far better to accept what was his and make the best of it.

''For now I would settle for a measure of contentment,'' he said firmly.

The Vicar abruptly raised his glass. ''Then that is what we shall strive for. Into battle, my son.''

Chapter Seven

Addy was miserable.

The slippers that until tonight had fitted perfectly now pinched her toes. The lace of her rose gown made her skin itch and the clips holding her raven curls were giving her a headache.

Even the lovely aromas drifting from the supper room were making her nose twitch in distaste.

Absurd, really.

The elegant soiree was precisely the sort of gathering that Addy enjoyed the most.

Unlike the previous ball, the townhouse was only modestly filled, with enough room to comfortably converse and move from one group to another. There was also a pleasantly relaxed atmosphere that displayed none of the usual spiteful gossip or fierce competition to outwit one another.

But while her host and hostess had been warmly delighted to meet her, and the other guests too polite to reveal their curiosity at the stranger in their midst, Addy was far from enjoying herself.

Rather than mingling with the others and becoming acquainted with the numerous young ladies scattered about the room, she discovered herself standing in a far corner.

Worse, she realized her narrowed gaze was unable to leave the tall, dark form of her husband.

Perhaps not so surprising, she told herself with an unmistakable twinge of annoyance.

From the moment they had swept into the room he had been besieged by a bevy of beautiful ladies. No, not besieged, she silently corrected. Mauled.

Her eyes narrowed a fraction further as she noted the delicate blonde that currently clung to one arm while a Titan-haired, full-bodied widow tenaciously sank her claws into the other.

They appeared to be a pair of ornaments that had permanently attached themselves to his side.

Not that Adam seemed distressed at their forward manner, she seethed. In truth he appeared infuriatingly content to laugh at their witty comments, to lean downward to whisper softly in their ears, and watch in fascination as they batted their lashes and pouted their sultry lips.

It was a sickening display. Utterly shameless.

For nearly half an hour she had awaited Adam to signal his distress. But in all that time he never once attempted to free himself from their grasp. There were no desperate glances about the room to plead for silent rescue. No polite hints that he would rather be in a pit of hot tar than captured by rabid females. Rather he appeared remarkably satisfied with his lot.

He also appeared to have forgotten her very existence.

Wiggling her toes, Addy cursed her pinching slippers, the itchy lace, the evil hair clips, and her suddenly unpredictable husband.

How was she suppose to enjoy the soiree with such annoyances?

As if sensing her simmering temper, Mr. Humbly suddenly appeared at her side, bringing with him two glasses of champagne and his soothing smile.

"Ah, Addy. I wondered where you had disappeared to."

Attempting to hide her discomfort, Addy forced her lips to curve in what she hoped was a smile.

"Are you enjoying your evening, Mr. Humbly?"

"Very much. So much nicer to be able to breathe and not have one's toes crushed by large matrons." He shot her a rather wicked glance. "Of course, I do miss the monkey."

Addy couldn't prevent a small chuckle. The Vicar was such a dear man.

"Perhaps Lord Umberly will attend. He is said to go everywhere with a parrot upon his shoulder."

"Ah, a treat indeed." He held out one of the glasses. "I brought you some champagne."

"Thank you." Addy took a small sip of the golden bubbles, but they landed heavily upon her coiled stomach.

"I pray that you do not intend to hover in the corner all evening, my dear."

She instinctively shied from his accusation. It smacked far too closely of cowardice.

"I am not hovering in the corner."

Humbly pointedly glanced about their remote location. "No?"

Addy gave a small sniff. "I am merely enjoying watching the various guests."

"Forgive me, my dear, but when I approached you did not appear to be particularly enjoying yourself. Indeed, you looked as if you had just bit into an unripe grape."

An unripe grape, indeed, she seethed. His toes did not ache. His skin did not itch. He did not have clips pricking his scalp or a husband being devoured by a group of harpies.

"That is absurd."

"Perhaps," he murmured, although there was a distinct twitch to his lips. "What do you think of our host?"

She lifted a vague shoulder. "Both Mr. and Mrs. Bates are very gracious."

"Yes. I understand Mr. Bates is an old friend of Adam. They seem very dissimilar, but then opposites often are attracted to one another."

Addy had been surprised herself to discover that Mr. Bates was a large, extroverted gentleman with a ready laugh. Not at all like Adam.

Perhaps Mr. Humbly had a point. The differences between the two might easily have drawn them together. Dark and light. A pity the same notion did not seem to have a similar effect between a husband and wife.

"Yes, I suppose."

"And I believe that is Mr. Bates's sister with Adam, is it not?"

Addy's teeth ground together as her gaze shifted to the tiny blonde plastered against her husband.

"I believe so."

"She is very lovely."

"She is passable in an insipid manner."

"No doubt she has been acquainted with Adam since they were both young."

Addy thought of Mrs. Hall's warnings of how the maiden had pursued Adam for years. Her hands clenched.

"I really could not say. Adam has never spoke of Mr. Bates or his sister."

Not appearing to notice her catty tone, Humbly studied the trio across the room.

"I wonder who the beautiful woman with the Titan hair is?"

"Mrs. Wilton," Addy retorted in clipped tones. She had detested the woman on sight. "She is a widow."

"Ah. She also seems to be a close acquaintance of Adam."

Close? She had practically crawled on top of him.

"Yes."

"Shall we join them?"

"No," Addy swiftly refused. "I would not wish to intrude."

"Intrude?" Humbly questioned in puzzlement.

Addy's features unknowingly hardened.

"Adam is clearly enjoying himself. I do not believe that I have ever seen him so delighted."

"Well, it is only polite to enjoy oneself at such an event," the Vicar murmured, not appearing to notice the outrageous antics of the two women.

"It appears Adam agrees with you," she said dryly.

"Addy, what a delightful surprise," a male voice intruded into their conversation.

With a faint sense of dread Addy turned to discover Lord Barclay standing at her side. He was as elegant as ever in his brilliant crimson coat with his golden hair shimmering in the candlelight. A gentleman that would trip the heart of any lady.

But Addy was in no mood to have her heart tripped. Nor did she desire to bandy words with a skilled rake.

Not when she needed to keep a close watch on those treacherous jades.

"Good evening, my lord," she forced herself to murmur politely.

"And Vicar Humbly." Lord Barclay swept a bow in the direction of her companion.

"My lord." Humbly performed his own awkward bow, then straightening he flashed Addy a gentle smile. "If you will excuse me I believe that I shall seek out the supper room."

Lord Barclay raised his quizzing glass to watch the older

gentleman amble away, his handsome features set in mocking lines.

"Gads, I believe the old fool should give the supper room an occasional miss," he drawled. "He grows more fat each occasion I see him."

Addy grew rigid at the unkind words. She could never abide those who poked fun at others.

"Mr. Humbly is a very kind and decent gentleman. He is also a guest in my house."

Swiftly realizing he had erred in his strategy, Lord Barclay summoned his powerful charm.

"Forgive me. I suppose he is a good enough sort, at least for a vicar. He possesses the sense not to preach at one or constantly frown in disapproval."

Addy was far from appeased. "I find him a delightful companion."

"Enough of Humbly." The nobleman waved an impatient hand. "I am far more interested in you. How glad I am that Foley convinced me to join him for this evening. I presumed it would be deadly dull, but now I find myself in debt to my persuasive friend."

"Indeed?"

"Yes. To think I have been given yet another opportunity to gaze upon your beauty. It seems I am uncommonly fortunate."

"Very pretty," she muttered.

"You do not believe that I am sincere?" he demanded, stepping close enough for his sleeve to brush the bare skin of her arm. Ridiculously Addy felt no more than irritation at his proximity. There were certainly none of the searing tremors that Adam could create with a mere glance lately. Odd, considering Lord Barclay was precisely the sort of gentleman she had always thought she preferred. "I assure you that I was quite disappointed when we were so rudely interrupted upon the last occasion."

Addy cast him a wary gaze, wondering if he were deliberately attempting to remind her of the embarrassing scene between herself and Adam.

"I believe we had come to the end of our conversation."

"No, Addy, do not speak of endings," he protested. "This is only a beginning."

"A beginning of what?" she asked bluntly.

He slowly smiled. "Whatever you desire."

She gave a shake of her head. "I hope you have not forgotten that I am a married woman?"

He flinched, lifting a dramatic hand to his heart. "How could I forget such a ghastly tragedy? Still your usually tenacious husband appears to be adequately entertained for the moment. Why should you not seek your own pleasure? Come with me to the gardens."

Returning her attention to Adam, Addy sucked in a sharp breath. Mrs. Wilton had actually placed one hand on his chest to lightly stroke the lapel of his coat.

"Addy."

The buzz of an unwelcome male voice in her ear made her impatiently turn toward her companion.

"I beg your pardon?"

A golden brow arched at her flashing black gaze. "I asked if you would join me for a turn in the garden."

"No. No, thank you."

His gaze slowly narrowed, clearly sensing the source of her prickly irritation.

"I thought you had more pride than to stand here like a neglected wallflower, Addy."

He managed to say precisely the wrong thing and Addy retreated behind a wall of icy disapproval. She did not need this man telling her that she was acting like a nodcock. She was quite intelligent enough to reason that out all on her own.

"If you will excuse me, I believe I shall join Mr. Humbly."

With her nose high in the air, Addy swept away. Neglected wallflower, indeed, she silently seethed.

The devil take all gentlemen.

And while he was at it, he could have overly forward minxes who clearly had no business attending soirees if they couldn't keep their claws off other women's husbands.

Blast it all.

It was well past two in the morning when Adam finished reading his latest notes from the War Department.

He could not deny a flare of guilt at neglecting his duties. Although he was merely a consultant and not directly involved in the final decisions that determined the course of the war, he knew that his word carried a great deal of weight. They depended upon his insight and years of study of battle strategies. They also depended on his firm refusal to become embroiled in the tedious political factions that created such discord among those who should be united.

And yet for all his sensible understanding that he was needed by his country, he did not completely regret the time he had devoted to his wife.

A faint smile curved his lips as he made his way from his study.

There had been no mistake that Addy had been thoroughly and utterly furious earlier this evening. Standing across the room she had never allowed her heated gaze to stray from the sight of Mrs. Wilton and Miss Bates as they had vied for his attention. Not even the appearance of that damnable Lord Barclay had been able to ease her annoyance.

It had been worth the irritation of having the two women flagrantly attempting to seduce him. It had even been worth devoting an entire evening to mindless chatter and shallow flirtations.

Surely Addy could not be so obviously angered without feeling something for him? Even if it was just possession.

Yes, he told himself as he started down the hall, it had been a profitable evening.

Heading for the stairs, Adam had passed by the closed door of the library when he noticed a faint glow of light.

Wondering who the devil could be up at such an hour he shoved open the door and stepped into the room. His surprise only deepened when he caught sight of Addy seated in a wing chair attired in nothing more than a sheer robe with her glorious hair woven into a simple braid.

His gaze narrowed as the dancing light from the fire played over her body, revealing a warm hint of the beauty beneath that robe.

A hungry, dangerous heat swept through his body at the sight of her lush curves.

He should leave, he told himself as the muscles of his groin began to stir. His need to lay with his wife was growing to a nearly painful ache. Only the inner determination to slowly and thoroughly seduce Addy until she begged for his touch kept him from sweeping her into his arms and taking her to his bed for the next week. Or perhaps the next month. There would be no more nights of her lying beneath him with stiff martyrdom.

Taking a step backward Adam was abruptly halted from his strategic retreat when Addy turned to regard him with a startled gaze.

''Adam.''

More or less trapped, Adam determinedly reined in his fierce desire and forced himself to move toward the center of the room. Surely he could conduct a pleasant conversation with his wife without tugging her onto the carpet and drowning in her sweetness?

"What are you doing up at this hour, Addy?"

She gave a vague shrug, her fingers toying with a ribbon upon her robe.

"I could not sleep."

"I saw the light beneath the door and feared that Mrs. Hall had forgotten to snuff out the candles." He moved closer, attempting to ignore the unmistakable silhouette of her body beneath the sheer material. "Is something troubling you?"

"No, of course not." She made a poor attempt at a smile. "I was just feeling rather restless."

A sudden flare of triumph rushed through Adam. Of course. She was still troubled by the events of the evening. Perhaps Humbly was not thoroughly noddy after all.

"Are you certain?" he probed with seeming innocence. "You were very quiet on the way home."

"Was I?"

"Yes. As if you had something upon your mind. Did Lord Barclay say anything to upset you?"

She gave a startled blink. "We spoke only briefly."

"Well, I could not help but notice that you left him quite abruptly and that he had a very petulant expression upon his countenance."

Without warning the dark eyes narrowed. "I am surprised that you managed to notice anything at all."

Adam sternly controlled his quivering lips. "I beg your pardon?"

"You seemed very preoccupied," she retorted in a tone that could only be described as snippy.

"I was merely keeping myself entertained, as you requested," he said mildly. "It was my understanding that you did not wish me to bother you during such events."

A faint color touched her cheeks. "Yes, well, you were certainly being entertained."

"Addy, you are not jealous, are you?" he demanded.

We'd Like to Invite You to Subscribe to Zebra's Regency Romance Book Club and Give You a Gift of 4 Free Books as Your Introduction! (Worth $19.96!)

If you're a Regency lover, imagine the joy of getting **4 FREE Zebra Regency Romances** and then the chance to have these lovely stories delivered to your home each month at the lowest price available! Well, that's our offer to you and here's how you benefit by becoming a Regency Romance subscriber:

- **4 FREE Introductory Regency Romances are delivered to your doorstep (you only pay for shipping and handling)**

- **4 BRAND NEW Regencies are then delivered each month (usually before they're available in bookstores)**

- **Subscribers save almost $4.00 every month**

- **You also receive a FREE monthly newsletter, which features author profiles, discounts, subscriber benefits, book previews and more**

- **No risks or obligations...in other words, you can cancel whenever you wish with no questions asked**

Join the thousands of readers who enjoy the savings and convenience offered to Regency Romance subscribers. After your initial introductory shipment, you receive 4 brand-new Zebra Regency Romances each month to examine for 10 days. Then, if you decide to keep the books, you'll pay the preferred subscriber's price, plus shipping and handling.

It's a no-lose proposition, so return the FREE BOOK CERTIFICATE today!

Say Yes to 4 Free Books!
Complete and return the order card to receive this $19.96 value, ABSOLUTELY FREE!

If the certificate is missing below, write to:
Regency Romance Book Club
P.O. Box 5214, Clifton, New Jersey 07015-5214
or call TOLL-FREE 1-800-770-1963
Visit our website at www.kensingtonbooks.com.

FREE BOOK CERTIFICATE

YES! Please rush me 4 Zebra Regency Romances (I only pay for shipping and handling). I understand that each month thereafter I will be able to preview 4 brand-new Regency Romances FREE for 10 days. Then, if I should decide to keep them, I will pay the money-saving preferred subscriber's price for all 4...that's a savings of 20% off the publisher's price. I may return any shipment within 10 days and owe nothing, and I may cancel this subscription at any time. My 4 FREE books will be mine to keep in any case.

Name _____

Address _____ Apt. _____

City _____ State _____ Zip _____

Telephone ( ) _____

Signature _____ RN102A
(If under 18, parent or guardian must sign.)

Terms and prices subject to change. Orders subject to acceptance by Regency Romance Book Club.
Offer valid in U.S. only.

There was a sharp silence as her eyes widened. It was obvious that the thought she might actually be jealous did not sit well with Addy.

"I am merely astonished that supposedly well-bred ladies would behave in such a shocking manner."

"Are you referring to Mrs. Wilton?"

He could almost hear her teeth grind.

"Her and Miss Bates. They were practically standing atop you."

Adam gave an inward shiver at the memory. Although he possessed enough natural vanity to appreciate being admired by a beautiful woman, he did not enjoy being battled for by two shallow, decidedly greedy vixens who viewed him as little more than a wealthy prize.

Even now his nose wrinkled at the clouds of perfume that had choked the air and the sharp talons that had dug into his arms.

"Surely you exaggerate, my dear?"

"Do you deny that they were flirting outrageously?" she demanded in a dangerous voice.

He met her gaze squarely. "No more outrageously than Lord Barclay flirts with you."

Her mouth opened then closed then opened once again before she managed to speak. Adam fiercely hoped that she did feel a measure of the same discomfort he had felt at seeing her with the golden haired lecher.

"I thought that they made an embarrassing spectacle of themselves," she at last muttered.

"Perhaps it is my turn to ask if you trust me," he charged softly.

She held his gaze for a long moment, then without warning she rose from the chair and paced toward the darkened windows. Adam caught his breath at the graceful sway of her hips. He could almost feel his hands running along those soft curves.

"As you said, our marriage is one of convenience not affection," she said in careful tones. "You might very well be attracted to another."

His feet were carrying him across the carpet before he could halt the movement. As much as he might secretly take pleasure at the thought of Addy burning with jealousy, he could not allow her to believe he would ever betray her trust.

He halted directly behind her, his gaze stroking the rigid set of her profile.

"No, I am not attracted to Mrs. Wilton or even Miss Bates," he assured her firmly. "I far prefer raven haired, midnight-eyed minxes."

He could feel her muscles tense as she slowly turned to face him.

"You are merely saying that."

"No, it is true, Addy." His hand rose to softly stroke her cheek. "Do you recall when you use to paint the old ruins on the edge of your property?"

Her lips softly parted. "Yes."

Adam found himself becoming lost in the soft darkness of her eyes. "I could see you from my window. I would stand there in fascination as the wind would blow your hair and your bright skirts would dance about you."

"You told me that I looked like a hoyden."

"No, you looked beautiful," he said with a husky sincerity, fiercely regretting his foolish words. He had told himself that he was only being sensible, that his wife must be utterly proper and demur. But he was beginning to fear his motives were not nearly so pure. "But you were also very wild and free. I suppose I thought I must tame you or you would slip from my grasp."

"I thought I was an embarrassment to you."

This vibrant, beautiful woman an embarrassment? His heart felt as if it were being clenched by a ruthless fist.

"Never that, Addy," he muttered, his hands smoothing over the satin skin of her face before moving to undo the braid and allowing her hair to tumble freely about her shoulders. "You are so lovely."

As if sensing the growing heat that shimmered in the air, Addy regarded him with wide eyes.

"Adam."

His fingers trailed through the raven curls, stirring to life the maddening scent of lilacs.

"This hair drives me mad," he whispered.

A pink tongue reached out to touch her lips. "It is very common. Not at all like Mrs. Wilton's red hair."

He gave a husky laugh. "Then why did I not spend the evening longing to see it tugged free and falling about her shoulders?"

Her gaze narrowed slightly. "She would not have objected."

"But you would have, eh, Addy?"

There was a long silence before she gave a sigh. "Yes."

"Good." Nearly trembling with the powerful urge to sweep her into his arms and remove all doubts as to where his passions lay, Adam lowered his head and claimed a brief, searing kiss. Her lips instinctively parted in seductive promise, making Adam's muscles tighten with a sharp, clamoring need. One tug, he told himself. One tug and she would be upon the carpet with his demanding body covering her soft form. Every quivering inch of him urged him to plunge into the desire arcing between them, but the rigid control that had ruled his life came to his belated rescue. With a deep groan he reluctantly lifted his head. She was still not certain of him. Still not capable of surrendering herself completely. Gazing down at her bemused expression he softly brushed a stray curl from her cheek. "Do not stay up too late, my dear."

Turning and walking away was the most difficult thing
Adam had ever done.

Only the knowledge that when Addy did come to him
eagerly and without reservation that it would be the most
glorious experience of his life kept him from tossing her
over his shoulder and taking her to his bed.

Patience.

He groaned as he stepped through the door.

Chapter Eight

"This one, I believe," Mr. Humbly announced, pointing to one of the numerous sketches spread across the table.

Addy smiled in satisfaction. The sketch was a simple one with Mr. Humbly seated in a casual manner with his uniquely sweet smile upon his lips.

"That is the one that I prefer as well," she said. "It is dignified without being pretentious."

Folding his hands across his belly, Humbly gave a knowing nod of his head. "I knew that I could depend upon you, Addy. This is precisely what I desired."

Addy felt a flustered heat rise to her cheeks. It was strangely uplifting to know that she had not disappointed this dear man.

"This is only the vaguest sketch," she felt compelled to warn. "There is still a great deal of work to be done."

The Vicar heaved a deep sigh. "I feared that you might say that."

Addy could not help but laugh at his expression of martyrdom. He might very well have passed as Daniel being fed to the lions.

"Do not worry. I shall ensure that Cook has plenty of lemon tarts on hand."

His expression miraculously lightened at the mention of his favorite treats.

"And perhaps a few of those almond cakes? I do adore those."

"Is there anything you do not adore?" she teased.

Humbly abruptly grimaced. "Cucumber sandwiches."

"Then I shall make very certain that they never appear on the tea tray."

He reached out to gently pat her hand. "Most thoughtful of you, my dear."

Picking up the chosen sketch, Addy briefly contemplated the work that still lay ahead of her. Work that sent a thrill of excitement through her, and gave her a reason to look forward to each day.

"It will take a few days to transfer the sketch to the canvas," she concluded. "And then I shall have to acquire the necessary supplies."

"Of course," Humbly readily agreed. "That will give me an opportunity to visit the Bishop. I suppose I have put it off long enough."

Addy lifted her brows at the unmistakable hint of reluctance in his voice.

"You do not appear particularly pleased."

"Oh, the Bishop is a fine gentleman," the Vicar was swift to assure her. "Quite a formidable scholar and a worthy leader of the Church. There are few men that I admire more."

"Then what troubles you?"

Humbly gave a rather sad shake of his head. "Somehow, no matter what my age, I always feel like a student being called to the headmaster's office."

Addy felt a twinge of sympathy for the poor man. She

knew all too well the sinking feeling of approaching a dominating personality. Did she not cringe when she was forced to call upon Adam each morning in the library?

Not any longer, a renegade voice whispered in the back of her mind.

The resentful, simmering anger that she always associated with Adam had slowly been tempered over the past few days. It was odd. Unexplainable. But she could not deny that while she still trembled when her husband was near, it had nothing to do with annoyance. Instead there was a breathless, shimmering magic that flooded through her body.

Against her will the image of their embrace from the evening before rose to her mind.

She had been so furious at the forward manner of Mrs. Wilton and Miss Bates. And even more so by Adam's seeming enjoyment of their blatant advances.

But her anger had swiftly turned to a searing need when Adam had taken her lips in a demanding kiss.

For a mindless moment she had longed to press close against him. To beg him to end the frantic ache that clenched deep inside her.

An ache that had lingered far into the night and still left her feeling restless and on edge.

Pressing an unconscious hand to her stomach, Addy battled to control her shameful thoughts.

Good heavens, she would soon be as bad as Mrs. Wilton with her seductive smiles and pleading glances.

Hoping that the Vicar would not notice the revealing heat in her cheeks, Addy awkwardly cleared her throat.

"It cannot be so bad," she at last managed.

"Oh, I assure you it is," Mr. Humbly insisted with a peculiar glint in his eyes. "On the last occasion the Bishop visited the Vicarage I managed to spill an entire pot of tea in his lap and no doubt permanently maimed him when I tripped upon the stairs and sent the both of us tumbling to the bottom.''

Thankfully distracted, Addy gave a choked laugh. ''Oh, goodness.''

''There is just something so horridly intimidating about the man,'' Humbly rued.

''Yes.'' Addy gave a small grimace. ''It is not pleasant to feel like an awkward child.''

''Precisely.'' Humbly suddenly smiled. ''Still, I can not ignore my duty. I just must ensure that I do not hold anything sharp in my hands. Thus far I have avoided actually stabbing the poor man.''

''I am certain you will be as gracious and charming as ever,'' Addy said.

''You are a good child.''

The sound of the door to the salon being pushed open interrupted them and both turned to watch the housekeeper enter and place a large tray on the table next to the sofa. Straightening, the servant turned to Addy with a wooden expression.

''Your tea, Mrs. Drake.''

''Thank you, Mrs. Hall.'' Addy moved forward. ''Is Mr. Drake still at home?''

Mrs. Hall shot her an oddly wary gaze. ''I believe he is upstairs, although he requested not to be disturbed.''

Addy frowned in surprise. It was strange enough that Adam had not yet left for the day. What could he possibly be doing that would demand he not be interrupted?

''That will be all,'' she at last murmured in distracted tones.

Pausing long enough to offer Mr. Humbly a chastising frown, the housekeeper turned to make her way from the room. Once alone Mr. Humbly moved to stand at Addy's side.

''I fear that Mrs. Hall does not entirely approve of me.''

Addy waved a dismissive hand. "You must forgive her. She has ludicrously concluded that Adam's odd behavior is somehow connected to your visit."

"Oh?" The Vicar raised his bushy brows. "Is Adam behaving oddly?"

"Surely you have noticed?" she demanded in surprise. Not even this vague, rather unworldly gentleman could fail to have noticed the changes in her husband. Especially after last evening. Her features hardened. Although Adam had assured her that he had no interest in the harpies, she was still infuriated by their reprehensible behavior. "He was allowing those women to flirt with him as if he were a common rogue."

"Certainly he was being polite, but a rogue?" Humbly protested with a searching gaze.

Addy wrapped her arms about her waist. "You can not deny that he did nothing to discourage those . . . women."

Humbly's smile became wry. "I do not believe that they were in need of encouragement."

"No," she retorted in clipped tones. "They were shameless."

"Addy, you can hardly lay the blame for their behavior upon poor Adam. What gentleman could possibly hope to stop a determined lady?"

She could not deny the truth in his words. The women had latched onto him with grim determination. It would have taken a team of oxen to pry them loose.

But while she might logically be able to dismiss the fleeting encounter, a dark, rather unpleasant part of her still brooded upon the memory.

It was little wonder that Adam had accused her of being jealous.

Addy stiffened in shock. No. It was not possible. To be jealous would imply she cared for her husband.

A husband she had not wanted and who furthermore possessed no feelings for her, she reminded herself sternly.

Disconcerted by her unwelcome thoughts she gave a sharp shake of her head. It was no more than a dislike for the women's lack of common decency, she tried to reassure herself. And a perfectly reasonable expectation for her husband to avoid creating undue gossip.

She was far from comforted by the hollow, surprisingly priggish explanation, but it was preferable to digging too deeply into her confused maze of emotions.

"He need not have appeared to be enjoying himself quite so enthusiastically," she retorted weakly.

A disturbing amusement suddenly glowed in the sherry eyes.

"Well, at least he was not being dull or overbearing," he murmured.

Possessing a sneaking suspicion that he was laughing at her, Addy's brows snapped together.

"What is that supposed to mean?"

"Nothing. I should change before I call upon the Bishop." The Vicar offered a hasty bow. "Excuse me."

Still frowning Addy watched her guest scurry from the room.

What the devil was Humbly implying?

That she would prefer her husband to devote his evenings to drink and women?

That was ridiculous.

Granted she had complained of Adam's rigid habits and his lack of interest in anything beyond war strategies. And perhaps she had secretly longed for him to be more dashing.

But . . .

Addy bit her lower lip.

But, what?

Adam was obviously attempting to loosen his stiff composure to please her. He was even attending social events that she knew he despised.

Surely his efforts should bring her pleasure?

The very fact he was suddenly considering her feelings at all was a miracle.

But Addy knew deep inside she was not pleased.

No. She was not pleased at all.

Adam felt like a young boy.

Or at least how he would imagine a young boy would feel if he had not possessed a father who sternly forbade any childish antics.

With a barely contained sense of anticipation he slipped through the hallways, ushering merchants through side doors, and carrying crates to the storeroom that he had commanded to be cleaned and refurbished.

He had never before attempted to surprise another and he was rather startled to discover just how pleasurable it was.

In truth he could barely restrain his impatience as he ordered the footmen to unload the crates and the maids to finish hanging the curtains that matched the pale rose sofa and chairs.

Only when he was certain that all was in readiness did he allow himself to make his way to the front salon.

Entering the room he briefly feared that Addy had returned to her chambers or perhaps even left the house all together. He felt a sharp stab of disappointment, then his gaze suddenly discovered her lovely form in a corner chair where she was closely studying the sketch she held in her hand.

He paused for a moment to simply drink in her beauty.

Seated beside the window she was bathed in golden sunlight. The raven hair shimmered with the dark luster of polished ebony. Her skin glowed with a flawless perfection and the sheer muslin gown draped to her curves . . .

No.

Adam brought an abrupt and firm end to the dangerous thoughts.

Heaven knew he had tormented himself enough through the night with images of those curves. He did not think his nerves could bear much more temptation.

Forcing himself to recall his reason for seeking out his wife, Adam stepped forward.

"Addy, may I have a moment?"

Glancing up in surprise she set aside her sketch. "Of course. What is it?"

"I have something I wish you to see."

It was not unexpected that she appeared taken aback by his request. "Very well," she agreed at last, slowly rising to her feet.

Offering his arm, Adam waited for Addy to place her fingers upon his sleeve lightly before leading her out of the room and up the staircase. For a time they moved in silence, then as he steered her toward the end of the long hall she shot him a questioning glance.

"Where are we going?"

"You shall see," he murmured, not halting until they reached the end of the hall. Lifting his hand he pushed open the door and waved her inside. "In here."

Her brows drew together in puzzlement. "Is this not a storage room?"

"It was."

She studied his well-guarded countenance for a long moment before slowly stepping into the room. Adam followed closely behind, watching her delicate countenance as she came to an abrupt halt.

Not even aware that he was holding his breath, Adam tensely waited as she gazed about the room. With wide eyes she studied the long shelves filled with every art supply that could be purchased in London, the pretty furnishings grouped close to the fireplace, and the stacks of canvases placed in a distant corner.

"Oh," she at last murmured, an unmistakable glow upon her face.

Releasing the breath he held, Adam felt a warm burst of satisfaction rush through him.

"What do you think?" he asked softly.

Her eyes were filled with wonder as she turned to face him. "You did this?"

He smiled faintly. "Yes."

"Why?"

"You are clearly in need of a place to work upon your portrait," he said, although in truth he knew that the real reason was that he longed to see her face light with happiness. He missed the vibrant, spirited minx she had been before their marriage. He missed her smile. At the moment, however, he did not wish to make demands upon their fragile relationship. It was far better that his offer appear one of generosity rather than a need to regain what he had unwittingly destroyed. "I thought you would prefer a space that will be yours to do as you please."

She gave a shake of her head. "I do not know what to say."

Rather uneasy at his unaccustomed role as benefactor, Adam waved a hand toward the shelves.

"I only purchased the most basic supplies, since I have little notion what an artist requires to paint her masterpiece."

She gave a sudden chuckle, her beautiful features luminous in the afternoon sunlight.

"It appears that you have acquired enough supplies for a dozen portraits."

The world screeched to a halt.

"You are pleased?"

"I . . ." She turned to meet his searching gaze, her words lost upon her parted lips.

"What?"

"I just never expected anything like this," she at last admitted. "It is very thoughtful."

A portion of his happiness dimmed. "You did not believe I was capable of being thoughtful?"

Her eyes darkened with dismay. "I did not mean that."

"Forgive me, Addy." He gave a rueful grimace. "In truth I have given you little reason to suppose I am a considerate husband."

She stepped closer, placing a hand on his arm. "That is not true. You have always been very generous. Both to me and my family."

He gave a shake of his head, his hand covering her own. "I am not speaking of money. I should have been more sensitive to the knowledge you were alone in this house with no one to ease your isolation."

Her features seemed to magically soften. "Well now I shall be very busy, indeed."

Adam glanced about the cheerful room. It was no wild meadow with a handful of ruins, but it had pleased her. And that was all he desired for the moment.

"And perhaps somewhat more content with your days," he suggested.

"Yes." She offered a tentative smile. "I am sure I shall be."

Adam felt his heart swell as he reached up to gently cup her cheek.

"That would please me very much."

Her eyes darkened as she gazed into his smiling countenance.

"Adam?"

"Yes?"

"Thank you."

"You are most welcome, my dear," he said in husky

tones, nearly overwhelmed by the urge to kiss her sweet lips.

Would she be shocked at being made love to by her husband in the middle of the day?

Or would she melt in his arms as she had done last evening?

Determined to discover, Adam was frustratingly interrupted when there was a knock on the door and a footman entered the room.

"Pardon me, sir."

Gritting his teeth Adam dropped his hand and stepped from his fiercely blushing bride. Hell and damnation. Would he ever get this woman in his bed?

"Yes?"

"A note has just been delivered for you." The young servant held out the folded paper, clearly embarrassed at having intruded at such an awkward moment.

Adam wryly grimaced as he reached for the note. It was not the footman's fault that he was finding it a delicate and nerve-wracking experience to seduce his own wife.

"Thank you." Waiting for the servant to slip from the room, Adam unfolded the paper and swiftly read the brief message. His heart sank as he realized it was imperative that he leave for the War Department. "Damn."

"What is it?" Addy demanded.

"It is from Liverpool."

"Is there trouble?"

"No." Adam shoved the note in his pocket and reached out to take her hand in his own. "But they have received dispatches from the Continent. He wishes me to come to his office to review them."

Although he was prepared for the hardening of her countenance and return of her wary distance, Adam felt a pang of disappointment.

Just for a moment there had been a true connection

between them. Her defenses had been lowered and he had been allowed to sense the vulnerable woman beneath her prickly composure.

Now he could not help but wonder if all his efforts were to be destroyed.

"Then you must go," she said in stiff tones.

Adam lifted a hand to rub the tense muscles of his neck. "We were suppose to attend the theater this evening."

She gave a faint shrug. "We shall go some other night."

"Yes." Knowing that he could not avoid his duty despite his desire to remain with Addy, Adam squared his shoulders. "I shall no doubt be very late."

The familiar air of disinterest settled about her like a shroud.

"Mr. Humbly will be here to keep me company."

Adam choked back a sigh of frustration. "I am sorry, Addy."

"Please, you must go," she said coolly.

Adam gave a nod of his head. There was really nothing left to say. Nothing that would ease the tension that was choking the air.

"I shall see you later."

Chapter Nine

Watching Adam leave the room, Addy instantly regretted her cold dismissal.

Lud, he had been so very kind, she silently chastised herself.

To think he would go to such an effort to surprise her with this lovely studio . . . it had touched her in a manner that she could barely express.

Never had anyone taken such care to please her.

Certainly not her parents who had always been far too concerned with their own pleasure to consider others. Or even her siblings who were as feckless and indifferent as their parents.

She had been nearly overwhelmed by the delight that had rushed through her when she had stepped into the room. She had not even known how to properly express her gratitude.

Then without warning the footman had intruded into their privacy and the tenuous peace that had momentarily bloomed between them was destroyed.

Addy had known precisely what the note would contain. She had also known that Adam would not decline the summons to make an appearance at the War Department.

What she had not expected was the sharp edged disappointment that had cut through her like a knife.

She had wanted him to toss the note in the fire. To gaze into her eyes and declare that he would remain at her side.

The fierce pang had frightened her with its intensity. Certainly she had always been annoyed by his decided preference to avoid her. What woman would not resent being ignored? But this . . . this struck perilously close to her heart.

In response she had discovered herself hastily retreating from the warmth between them. It had been utterly instinctive and it was not until Adam had wearily left the room that she had been struck by regret.

She had not meant to ruin his obvious overture. She wished that she had attempted to be more understanding.

And now it was too late.

Feeling restless and oddly dissatisfied, Addy discovered herself pacing the house. Moving from one room to another she sought some means of distracting her dark mood. She had to do something or go mad.

At last she called for the carriage and along with Mr. Humbly she set off for an afternoon of shopping. Surely being out of the house would help to ease her tension.

Dropping Mr. Humbly at a shop to replace his lost hat and cravats, Addy proceeded to the exclusive seamstress that she had discovered was all the rage. She hoped that choosing a new gown would lift her spirits.

Not surprisingly, the seamstress was anxious to please the wife of Mr. Drake.

Leaving her assistant with the clutch of debutantes admiring the latest bonnets, the rotund woman steered Addy to a counter where she had piled several bolts of material.

"What of this?" the seamstress purred, running a hand

over a delicate muslin material. "It is a lovely shade of peach."

It was lovely.

Elegant, subdued, and quite proper for a true lady.

Addy, however, was swift to shake her head in refusal.

She had an endless number of elegant, subdued and proper gowns. Without quite knowing why she suddenly longed for a brilliant, eye-catching gown. A gown that would stir the interest of the most indifferent gentleman.

The dangerous thought was swiftly squashed as Addy tapped an impatient finger upon the counter.

"I was thinking of something a bit bolder."

"Of course." The woman smiled in a knowing manner. "I believe that I have just the thing."

With a an efficient movement the seamstress disappeared from the room returning in a blink of an eye with a satin material in a deep shimmering blue.

Addy caught her breath in pleasure, reaching out to stroke the lovely material.

It was perfect.

"Yes."

"Perhaps with some military fobbing and brass buttons upon the pclissc?" thc woman suggested.

Addy gave a slow nod of her head, already visualizing the walking dress in her mind.

"I think that would be lovely."

A true businesswoman, the seamstress smiled in a coy manner.

"And a matching bonnet, of course."

Addy gave an inward shrug. There was little point in ordering a new gown if she did not have a bonnet to set it off.

"Of course," she said in decisive tones.

Folding the material, the seamstress casually glanced toward the back of the shop.

"I do have several new silks that would be perfect for a ball gown."

Addy gave a faint smile. "I shall return later in the week to view them."

"Very good. I shall have your new gown ready for a fitting."

"Thank you."

Pleased with her choice, Addy collected her reticule and made her way toward the door. She was forced to halt as a maid suddenly shoved the door open and an elegant Titan-haired woman swept into the shop.

Addy felt her heart drop to the tips of her toes as she recognized the lovely countenance of Mrs. Wilton.

Blast. Of all the people in London, this woman was the very last one she wished to encounter.

Still, her pride demanded that she not slink past the woman as if she were some cowardly schoolgirl. Instead, she squared her shoulders and met the glittering gaze as Mrs. Wilton halted before her.

"Mrs. Drake," the older woman exclaimed in mocking surprise.

Addy allowed a cold smile to touch her lips. "Mrs. Wilton."

"I certainly did not expect to encounter you here," the woman drawled.

"Really? I am told that Mrs. Manson is quite popular this season."

"She is, of course, but I thought that you did not care to leave your house."

Knowing Mrs. Wilton was deliberately attempting to get a rise out of her, Addy determinedly reined in her ready temper.

"I cannot imagine where you came by such a notion."

"Well, I have never seen you shopping or even visiting

about town. To tell the truth, there was a rumor that Adam kept you locked away.''

Addy tilted her chin in disdain. "How utterly ridiculous. Adam would never treat me with anything but the most tender care. Unlike many gentlemen, he is a most devoted husband.''

Her deliberate thrust slid home and Mrs. Wilton's countenance hardened. The spiteful vixen, however, was not about to be outdone.

''Then I suppose the nasty rumors that Adam spends his days at the War Department and his evenings at his club arc also untruc?''

Addy flinched, but her smile never faltered. Gads, but she wanted to slap the smug smile from the lovely face. Or perhaps wrench out a few of those suspiciously red curls.

"Quite untrue,'' she blatantly lied instead.

"If you say so,'' the woman mocked. "Although I suppose most abandoned wives would deny their husbands prefer the comfort of their clubs to the comfort of their marriage bed.''

First the slap, and then the hair, Addy silently plotted her strategy. And then maybe a kick to the rather wide derriere.

"I would think you have better things to do with your time than to gossip about my husband, Mrs. Wilton.''

The older woman shrugged. "It is difficult to avoid the latest scandals. And I will admit that I have always held a certain fondness for Adam. It broke my heart to learn that he had been forced into marriage with a woman he was ashamed to allow out the front door.''

"Adam is not ashamed of me,'' she said in icy, concise tones. "Although I do begin to comprehend his warning of not going about London on my own. There is no telling when or where one might stumble across some venomous creature.''

A dull flush darkened the thin countenance as Mrs. Wilton gave an angry sniff.

"Return to your townhouse, Mrs. Drake," she hissed. "Adam already avoids your company. It will not be long before he begins to seek a warm and willing lady to offer him companionship. A companionship that a petulant child could never offer."

With a toss of her head Mrs. Wilton continued into the shop, leaving behind an oddly shaken Addy.

Standing completely still she felt the breath slowly being leached from her body.

She should be laughing aside the woman's poisonous barbs, she told herself weakly. Mrs. Wilton had merely been striking out blindly in the hopes of distressing her. Such women were born troublemakers.

But oddly, Addy found it impossible to ignore the sharp words.

A petulant child . . .

The ugly words had struck a nerve deep within Addy.

Dear heavens, how could she deny such a charge when it was so painfully true?

With a blinding clarity she suddenly realized that she had behaved as a petulant child since her marriage to Adam. Perhaps not consciously, she thought, as she attempted to soothe her sudden bout of guilt. But there was no doubt she had been resentful and increasingly frigid over the past few months.

She had not desired to wed Adam. His arrogant commands of what he expected of his wife had only fueled her anger at being sacrificed for the sake of her family.

In turn she had determined to ensure that Adam fully realized she was his wife only under sufferance. She would make no effort to ease the strain between them. Or to seek a closer bond.

She found it ridiculous, in her anger, that she had never

stopped to think her behavior was creating as much discomfort for herself as for Adam. Or that she was willfully pushing him to seek solace from another.

A shudder swept through her body as she recalled her cold indifference to his presence in her bed.

How long would any gentleman tolerate such rebuffs before turning to the warmth of welcoming arms?

Warmth that was blatantly offered by women such as Mrs. Wilton?

A cold ball of fear settled in the pit of her stomach.

What had she been thinking about?

Or more to the point, not thinking about?

Even now Adam could be seeking a mistress to ease the need to be desired.

That could be the reason he had been acting so oddly. Adam was far too honorable to contemplate breaking his marriage vows without a few pangs of guilt.

"Addy. Addy, my dear, have you finished your shopping?"

With a blink, Addy allowed her gaze to focus upon the rumpled gentleman standing before her.

A hint of color touched her cheeks as she realized she had been standing at the door and staring at nothing like a common nodcock.

"Yes."

Firmly taking command of herself, Addy allowed the Vicar to escort her out of the shop and into the waiting carriage. Within moments they were plodding their way through the heavy London traffic.

Settling back in his seat, Mr. Humbly regarded her with a searching gaze.

"Was that not Mrs. Wilton in the shop?"

Addy curled her hands into tiny fists. "It was."

"What an odd coincidence."

Addy grimaced. "More unfortunate than odd."

"I hope she has not said anything to upset you?"

Addy knew she should hold her tongue, but the emotions that Mrs. Wilton had stirred to life were too much to contain.

"She upsets others by simply opening her mouth. She is a vile, unpleasant woman."

"No." Humbly gave a slow shake of his head. "I would say instead that she is a jealous, bitter woman."

His words caught Addy off guard. "Jealous? Of me?"

"Of course." The round countenance held a pensive expression. "By all reports her husband was nearly double her age and possessed a quarrelsome nature. It is also said that he drank heavily during the last few years of his life, commonly creating ugly scenes among society. Mrs. Wilton paid dearly to achieve her current status, while you were given a husband who is not only handsome, but of an even temperament. She no doubt feels that it is unfair that you have been so fortunate."

"I do hope that you do not expect me to sympathize with that jade," Addy retorted with a supreme lack of pity for the older woman. "She as good as announced she intended to seduce my husband."

Humbly gave a choked cough at her blunt words. "I would guess that Adam might have something to say about that."

Addy felt that cold ball once again in her stomach. "Yes."

"You do not sound so certain." The gray brows lowered into a frown. "Surely you trust Adam?"

"It is not that," she was swift to protest. "But Mrs. Wilton is very beautiful."

"Not nearly as beautiful as you."

"Thank you." Addy smiled with wry disbelief, knowing he was merely being kind. "Still I am not sophisticated or experienced enough in how best to keep a gentleman's interest."

"Addy, you are being absurd," Mr. Humbly chastised gently.

Addy sincerely hoped that she was. The mere thought of Adam lying in the arms of Mrs. Wilton was enough to make her feel as if she had been kicked by a very large, very angry mule.

"Am I?" she demanded, her eyes dark with her inner turmoil. "You saw Adam at the soiree. Perhaps he has grown bored with me."

"Bored? How could he possibly grow bored with a lovely, utterly enchanting bride?"

Addy's breath caught in her throat. "I am not always enchanting, I fear. Indeed, I . . ."

"Yes?"

She flushed as she realized she could not possibly admit her lack of response to Adam's touch.

"Nothing."

Leaning forward the Vicar gently patted her hand.

"You are fretting over nothing, my dear," he assured her firmly, then he offered her a sweet smile. "Now, shall we stop at Gunter's for a special treat?"

Adam felt weary to his very bones.

For the entire day he had been closeted with several cabinet members in a cramped office, poring over the packet of missives that had arrived. There had been the usual arguments, at times almost violent, as they attempted to sort through the success and failures of the troops. And, of course, the endless wrangling as they plotted the fresh orders that were to be sent.

Adam had discovered himself surprisingly short-tempered as the politicians had battled to gain the upper hand. More than once he wanted to damn them to the netherworld as they angled for the best means of furthering their own positions, rather than concerning themselves with the brave soldiers who were risking their lives.

The War Department was no place for ambition or greed, he had longed to shout over the babbling voices.

Only the knowledge that he was one of the few present who was genuinely dedicated to saving lives kept him from storming out in disgust.

Arriving home, Adam removed his hat and gloves, at the same time warning the footman he would return to the office within the hour. Then, making his way down the hall, he entered the library.

He had reached the center of the room before he belatedly realized he was not alone. Narrowing his gaze, he studied the sweetly curved form of his wife snuggled in a wing chair.

She looked all of twelve with her hair floating about her shoulders and her features relaxed in sleep, he thought, as he changed directions to stand before the chair. Then the flickering firelight captured the delectable curve of her breast that was revealed by the gaping robe and he rapidly revised his bemused thoughts.

No, this was no child.

She was a beautiful temptress who was nearly driving him mad with longing.

His body clenched with need even as he sternly reminded himself this was no time to lust after his wife.

Not when a room filled with powerful gentleman awaited his return.

Reaching out he stroked his hand over the satin darkness of her hair.

"Addy?"

"Mmm?"

He gave a soft chuckle. "Addy, wake up."

With obvious reluctance her eyes slowly opened and she regarded him with dazed confusion.

"Adam. What is it?"

"You seem to have fallen asleep in the library."

"Oh." Giving a faint shake of her head, Addy straightened in the chair. "Yes."

"Is there something wrong with your bedchamber?" he asked with a teasing smile.

She regarded him blankly. "No."

"Well, you appear to be spending a great deal of time sleeping in the library lately."

"Oh . . . yes." She raised a hand to push back her heavy curls. Flushed with sleep and barely dressed, she had never appeared so tempting. Adam felt a fierce tug deep inside him. "I wished to speak with you."

Adam raised his brows in surprise. "Tonight?"

"Yes."

He heaved a rueful smile. It seemed that fate was determined to keep the two of them at odds.

"Forgive me, Addy, but I have only returned to retrieve some papers I had forgotten. I must leave quite soon."

"At this hour?"

"Yes, we must send out the new dispatches tomorrow."

There was no mistaking the ripple of disappointment that crossed her countenance.

"I see."

"Do you?" Running a weary hand through his hair he gazed down at her shadowed eyes. How could he make her comprehend his clear if overwhelming duty? "Addy, there are thousands of young soldiers who are risking their lives every day. Each decision I make, each order that is dispatched has the potential to bring England glory or destroy the lives of hundreds. It is not a responsibility I can take lightly."

She appeared startled by his abrupt confession. "No, of course not."

"It is not easy." He grimaced. "Indeed, it is damnably frustrating."

"Frustrating?"

"I suppose the best way to explain it is to say that it is like playing a game of chess without being allowed to see the board," he admitted slowly, unaccustomed to discussing his efforts. "Strategy depends first and foremost on precise information. You must know the terrain, the weather, the estates or towns that can be depended upon to provide supplies, and of course, the precise location of the movement of the opposing forces."

She considered his words before giving a slow shake of her head.

"I had not realized that it was so terribly complicated."

"Not really complicated," he denied, "but it does involve a combination of information. Unfortunately it is impossible to maintain an adequate communication with our troops and the reports we receive are weeks out of date. Even worse, our maps are sadly lacking in the detail that I need. Even the most mundane hill or copse of trees can alter the battle."

Amazingly her expression softened to one of open sympathy. "I begin to realize the source of your frustration."

"I have not even mentioned the constant state of unrest in Spain; with no true leader and the generals compelled to protect their individual provinces, there can be no dependable force to aid our soldiers."

With a graceful motion Addy rose to her feet and placed a hand upon his arm.

"I am certain that you do your best, Adam," she said with a soft sincerity. "It is all that anyone can ask of you."

Profoundly aware of the heat and scent of her wrapping about him, Adam struggled to keep his hands at his side.

He dare not touch her.

Not now.

Not until he had hours, perhaps days to explore those lush curves with the exquisite care they deserved.

Gads, he wondered if he would have to request his valet to keep his hands tied behind his back! It seemed the only certain means of controlling his aching need.

"Forgive me, Addy. I did not mean to bore you with my complaints," he forced himself to speak, sternly forbidding his gaze to stray toward the bewitching neckline of her robe.

"I am not bored," she said with a startling insistence. "I wish you would have spoken of this sooner. I did not fully comprehend the vast responsibility you must bear."

He gave an uncomfortable shrug, hoping he had not painted himself as a hero. It was the men fighting the battles who deserved such a title.

"I am only one of many."

"Still, it must weigh heavily upon you."

"Yes, it does," he admitted lowly. "I can not help but attempt to second-guess our every decision. There are even times when I have debated traveling to the Continent so I can view the terrain for myself."

"No!" She denied in a sharp tone, startling them both with her ferocity. Then, clearly embarrassed by her emotional response, she gave a restless shrug. "I mean, I am certain you are more valuable here. There are many who can send the information to London. There are only a few who are so well versed in war strategies."

Adam gazed deep into the wide, midnight eyes, feeling a sudden surge of hope. Until this moment he would have presumed that Addy would be delighted to be rid of her tedious husband. Her fierce response was enough to fill his heart with warmth.

It was something to build upon, he assured himself.

"That is what the Prince tells me," he said with a slow smile. "That does not make it easier to remain so far from those who are sacrificing so much for their country."

"I suppose we must all contribute in the best way that we can," she said firmly.

Despite his best intentions, his hand rose to lightly brush her cheek.

"So wise, my dear."

A pained expression darkened her countenance. "No, not wise."

He determinedly tilted her chin upward to regard her pale features. "What is it?"

"I have been very selfish."

His brows snapped together. "Absurd."

"No, it is true," she insisted. "When you were gone so much I only considered the notion you preferred to be away from me. I did not take the time to realize there are so many who depend upon you."

It was precisely what Adam desired. At last it appeared Addy was willing to consider the obligation he felt toward the war. At the same time he could not allow her to shoulder the full blame.

He should have discussed his deep sense of duty. And of course, he should never have allowed himself to become so consumed with his work that Addy felt abandoned in the first place.

"You are not selfish, Addy," he assured her. "I have neglected you shamelessly. But after tomorrow I will be free once again to devote myself to you."

"No, you must concentrate on your duties."

He gave a shake of his head. "I will not forget my duties, but there is more to life than war. I have forgotten that for too long."

Silence descended, broken only by the crackle of the fire as she simply gazed at him. With a soft sigh Adam slid his arms about her and drew her close.

Damnation, holding her close felt so good, he thought with a sense of wonderment.

Indeed, he rather astonishingly realized that he could spend the rest of the evening simply holding her.

Laying her head against his shoulder, Addy gently cleared her throat.

"Adam?"

"Mmm?"

"Were you not leaving?"

He buried his face in the fragrant softness of her hair.

"In a moment."

"Adam?"

"You feel so good in my arms," he muttered.

"I do?"

She sounded absurdly surprised and he tightened his arms.

"Perfect. So sweet and soft. Gads, I could hold you like this forever."

There was another blissful silence before Addy lifted her head.

"Adam, you must go."

"Soon." He pressed her head back to his shoulder. "Soon."

Chapter Ten

The house was blissfully quiet.

With a significant tingle of anticipation, Adam folded his cravat into a neat knot.

The past week had been a delight. As he had promised Addy he had devoted little attention to the war efforts and instead concentrated his mind on his bride.

There had been walks in the park, nights at the theater, and one memorable musicale that had forced both Addy and Adam to flee the room before they erupted into whoops of laughter.

A delicate, precious bond had begun to develop over the days, but tonight was the first night that he and his wife would be completely alone.

An unconscious smile touched his lips as he recalled his inner elation when Humbly had casually announced his invitation to the Bishop's. At long last he would have an entire evening with Addy. An evening that he very much intended her to recall for the rest of her life.

Already his blood ran hot with suppressed desire. For the past week he had been forced to content himself with lingering touches and snatched kisses. With Humbly always hovering nearby it had been impossible to maneuver Addy alone.

But tonight . . .

His fingers fumbled slightly—with an eager motion his valet moved forward to offer his assistance.

"If I may suggest, sir . . ."

"No." With a smile, Adam halted the outstretched hands. "No Oriental. No Cascade. No Mailcoach. I will not appear the buffoon even for you, Dobson."

With obvious reluctance the valet stepped back. "Very well."

With an apologetic glance at his servant Adam returned to his efforts.

"Yes, I know I am the greatest trial. You must admit, however, that I have never requested you to gloss my boots with some ridiculous concoction nor forced you to pad my coats or bind me with corsets."

"I should think not," Dobson retorted with loyal outrage. "Your form is the envy of every gentleman in London."

"Hardly that," Adam denied, all too aware he was not the sort to strike envy in the heart of anyone. "But I do draw the line at primping like a dashed fop. You must content yourself with the knowledge I am a dull gentleman with no ambition to join the ranks of the dandies."

"I thank God every night you are not so inclined, sir," Dobson was swift to reassure him, then he gently cleared his throat. "But I did sense that you wished to appear at your best this evening."

Startled by his servant's perception Adam abruptly swung about to face him.

"Why the devil would you think such a thing?"

"Well . . ." Reddening slightly, Dobson glanced toward the bed covered with the numerous coats that Adam had discarded before settling upon a deep cinnamon coat with a striped waistcoat.

Adam grimaced at his unusual bout of vanity. "You have made your point. I am behaving like the veriest coxcomb. Rather ridiculous considering that I am merely spending an evening at home with my wife."

Dobson offered a faint smile. "What more important occasion is there?"

A delicious shiver raced through his body at the thought of the evening ahead.

"Ah, very true, Dobson. Gads, it has been too long since I have managed to have Mrs. Drake to myself."

"It is always awkward to have a guest constantly underfoot," the valet readily agreed.

Adam felt a swift stab of guilt at his unkindly desire for Humbly to disappear. Goodness knew that before his arrival an evening alone with Addy would have been a stiff, formal affair. Certainly he would not have been anticipating the thought of his wife happily chatting about their day together over dinner or counting the moments until he could gather her in his arms and kiss her senseless.

"Not that I grudge Humbly's visit," he forced himself to say with meticulous honesty. "He has managed to bring a bit of life to our tedious household. Still, I do appreciate his evening with the Bishop."

Dobson nodded in a knowing manner. "As will Mrs. Drake, I am sure."

"I do hope so," Adam murmured, recalling how her eyes had darkened and her lips parted when he had briefly kissed her earlier in the day. Although he was no experienced rake, he did know when a lady was responding to his touch. He was sure she was as anxious as he to succumb to their rising passions.

"She is a lovely lady, if I may be so bold," Dobson broke

into his delightful imaginings with a smile. "The staff is very devoted to her."

"Yes, she is lovely." Adam heard the faint sound of a gong. "And I have no desire to keep her waiting."

Fussily brushing the coat until he was certain no renegade bit of fluff dared to mar the perfection, Dobson stepped back and gave a nod.

"There."

Adam's lips twitched. "Will I do?"

"Exquisitely."

"Thank you."

Still smiling at his servant's absurd admiration, Adam made his way down the stairs. He encountered the house-keeper as she bustled from the library.

"Ah, Mrs. Hall, is Mrs. Drake down yet?"

With a smile that had been decidedly absent since the Vicar's arrival, the woman gave a nod of her head.

"Yes, sir. She is in the front salon."

"Thank you."

Feeling oddly nervous, Adam hurried down the hall and entered the salon. He discovered his wife standing beside the fireplace and his breath caught.

Accustomed to the pale, modest gowns he had chosen, he was caught off guard by the dazzling moss green satin that shimmered in the firelight. The rich color contrasted sharply with her pure white skin and the darkness of her thick curls, while the soft material offered a tantalizing hint of the curves beneath.

She looked daring and utterly beguiling.

He sucked in a sharp breath.

Perhaps hearing his instinctively male reaction, Addy slowly turned to regard him with a faintly shy smile.

"Good evening, Adam."

"Addy." He moved forward, not bothering to disguise his appreciative gaze. "What a beautiful gown."

Clearly uncertain what his reaction would be she breathed a soft sigh of relief. If it were possible, Adam would have kicked himself for convincing her she must have his approval for such a simple thing as choosing her own gowns.

What an arrogant ass he had been.

"Do you like it? The color is rather bold."

"You have never looked so beautiful," he said sincerely.

"Thank you." Adam was relieved when her wariness receded and a faintly teasing glint entered her dark eyes. "I suppose I should confess that I have purchased several more gowns and a countless number of bonnets."

He easily followed her lighthearted teasing. "Ah, there are no doubt matching slippers and gloves?"

"Of course, although I did limit myself to only five new fans."

"Will I be forced to give up my dressing room to make room for your numerous purchases?"

She gave a sudden chuckle. "I shall contrive to keep them contained to my own wardrobe."

He moved to lightly stroke a dark curl that lay against her cheek. "I am willing to sacrifice to see such a smile," he admitted, his lips twisting with a rueful humor. "And I am honest enough to admit that your sense of fashion is vastly superior to my own."

A soft blush rose to her countenance. "Nonsense."

"No, it is the simple truth," he admitted, then sensing her growing discomfort, he deliberately shifted the conversation. "How does your portrait go?"

Her expression immediately brightened. "Very well, despite the Vicar's grumbling at having to sit for so long. Poor Cook is forced to rise an hour early just to ensure that we have an ample supply of lemon tarts."

Adam gave an amused shake of his head at Humbly's passion for sweets.

"You have all the supplies that you need?"

"Yes, indeed," she swiftly assured him. "The studio is perfect."

"Good."

She glanced through her lashes in an almost coy manner. "I have never possessed such a place of my own. I feel shamelessly spoiled."

His hand shifted to cup her cheek, his gaze lowering to the tempting curve of her lips.

"Not spoiled, Addy, simply appreciated." The distracting lips parted at his soft words, but before he could take advantage of the unspoken invitation the reverberating sound of the second gong had him reluctantly pulling away. "Damn. I suppose we should go through."

A hint of devilment shimmered in her eyes. "Cook would be most disappointed if we allowed her meal to become cold."

Adam heaved a resigned sigh. "I feared you would say that." He held out his arm. "Come, we cannot have a mutiny in the kitchen."

Together they moved to the dining room, allowing themselves to be seated at the large mahogany table. It was an elegant room with tangerine walls and gilded cornices. Several fine Wedgwood platters were placed upon a side table along with sterling silver platters that had been collected by his family for generations.

Adam's only thought, however, was for the woman seated across from him as they partook of the various dishes. Although he fully appreciated her easy conversation and occasional teasing comments, he was anxious to finish the meal and have the opportunity to lure her to his chamber.

Indeed, it was near purgatory not to simply bolt down the food and toss her over his shoulder.

It was not until dessert was set before him that he took any notice of the food being set before him. Regarding the pale, smooth delicacy he lifted his head in surprise.

"Custard? Is this your doing?"

She appeared charmingly self-conscious. "I recalled you saying that it was a favorite of yours when you were young."

Adam felt his heart warm to her obvious effort to please him. It was a tangible symbol of the change in their relationship.

"Yes, indeed. My mother would often slip it up to my room when I had been banished by my father for some misdeed."

She gave a startled laugh at his confession. "I cannot imagine that happened very often."

The unwelcome image of his father's forbidding countenance rose to mind. Adam did not particularly desire to brood upon Franklin Drake tonight. The memories always held an edge of bittersweet pain.

"More times than I could possibly count," he grudgingly revealed. "My father had a wide definition of what constituted misbehavior."

"He was a very stern gentleman," she agreed softly.

"I do not believe I ever saw him smile."

"Never?"

Adam smiled wryly. "Not even when I surprised him with a picture I had painted of him for his birthday when I was just five."

"Oh, I am certain he must have appreciated your gift," she protested.

Adam's features unknowingly hardened. "Actually I was confined to my chamber for a week for dripping paint on my new coat."

Addy sucked in a sharp breath at his words. "That is horrid."

Realizing that he had revealed more than he had intended, Adam gave a restless shrug.

"My father strongly believed that offering indulgence to a child was destructive to their character."

"Balderdash!"

Adam gave a choked laugh at her fierce tone. "Yes, well, I suppose in his own way he was attempting to be a good father."

Addy did not appear to be appeased. Instead the dark eyes flashed with a surprising anger.

"He would have been a better father had he spent less time chastising you and more time simply appreciating what a fine son he possessed."

Adam was struck sharply by the motherly concern in her voice.

Good heavens, he had never thought of Addy as a mother. Oh, he had certainly considered the vague notion they would eventually have children. He was not a complete simpleton. But to actually imagine this woman heavy with his child . . . to think of her with a baby in her arms. It sent an indefinable emotion surging through his body.

He suddenly realized that he deeply desired children. And that he wanted this warm, wonderful woman to be their mother.

"As you would your own son?" he questioned in low tones.

Her spoon abruptly dropped onto the table with a loud clatter.

"I . . . yes, I hope I should be a loving mother," she said in flustered tones.

Adam leaned forward. "I do not doubt you will be a wonderful mother."

Her gaze abruptly lowered as a delightful warmth filled her cheeks.

"I have never really considered such a role."

"You do desire children, do you not?" he demanded with a faint frown.

"Of course."

Adam's smile suddenly returned as relief poured through

him. He realized he would have been fiercely disappointed if she had announced a dislike for carrying his child.

"Odd that we have never discussed the subject," he mused.

Clearly not entirely comfortable with the intimate turn of the conversation, her hands dropped to her lap.

"I suppose most couples simply assume there will be children."

"I should like to see our child in your arms," he told her gently.

Her napkin slipped to the floor. "I . . . It is difficult to imagine myself as a parent."

Adam gave a small chuckle, taking a great delight in her shy embarrassment. It revealed she was no longer stoically indifferent to the process of creating such children.

"You at least have the benefit of having a happy childhood," he said, hoping to ease her discomfort.

Slowly she raised her gaze to offer him a wry grimace. "Actually it was more chaotic than happy, I fear."

Adam was taken aback by the low words. Addy had always seemed so attached to her family. In truth, he had wondered if she would ever be truly happy being separated from her parents.

"But they love you," he insisted.

"In a very haphazard manner," she conceded. "More often than not they forgot they even possessed children. We could disappear for days without them ever realizing we were missing."

He searched her pale countenance with a faint puzzlement. "You always appeared quite content."

"Oh, I was not unhappy," she was quick to reassure him. "I possessed a great deal of freedom and I was encouraged to pursue my own interests. But there were times when I wished for a more stable environment."

Adam slowly smiled, wishing she were close enough to

touch. "Perhaps between the two of us we shall manage to discover a method between chaos and perfection."

A silence fell as their gazes tangled and that ready awareness sparked to life.

With a hasty motion Adam rose to his feet. Gads, he could wait no longer.

"Are you finished?"

"Yes." Pushing herself to her feet, Addy waited for him to take her hand and place it upon his arm. Together they moved out of the room and down the hall. Tilting back her head Addy offered him a teasing smile. "The house seems very quiet without Mr. Humbly."

"Yes, indeed. Who would have thought that one vicar could create such a difference in a household?"

"It has been lovely to have him about," she said hesitantly, as if uncertain whether Adam was as delighted as herself with their visitor.

"Oh, I agree. Not only is he a charming companion, he is far more wise than he would have others believe. In truth, he has a manner of forcing one to consider a situation from a viewpoint previously unnoticed."

She gave a startled blink at his dry words. "You, too?"

He chuckled as he steered her into the salon and firmly shut the door behind them.

"I think he is also a rather devious gentleman as well."

"But only with the best intentions."

"I do hope so." He gave a dramatic shudder. "I would not wish to think he would use such skills for nefarious purposes. London would not be safe."

"Perhaps we should send a note to the Bishop warning him to be on guard?" she questioned with a smile.

"Definitely not." Placing his hands upon her shoulders he gazed deep into her eyes. "I do not wish the Bishop to send Humbly back to us for several more hours."

Her breath quickened and her eyes darkened at his suggestive words. Adam felt his own body react to her ready response. There was no stiffness in her body, no resignation upon her sweet countenance. Instead, a delightful flush of excitement bloomed beneath her skin.

"I thought you enjoyed his company," she said in breathless tones.

"I do." He deliberately stepped forward, surrounding himself in her lilac heat. "Just not as much as I enjoy having an entire evening alone with my wife."

Her lips softly parted. "Oh."

"Especially when she is looking like a beautiful gypsy," he murmured.

A startling flare of uncertainty rippled across her expressive countenance.

"I am not beautiful."

Adam was baffled by her lack of confidence. How could she not know how lovely she was? Every gentleman in London would be at her feet if she chose to honor them with her warm smile.

Which was no doubt the reason he had virtually cloistered her in this house, an unwelcome voice whispered in the back of his mind.

He was swift to banish the renegade thought.

Tonight was a new beginning.

It was his opportunity to prove to her once and for all that she was utterly and thoroughly cherished.

"Yes, you are," he said gently, moving to take her hand and press it to his racing heart. "This is what you do to me when I gaze upon you."

She nervously wet her lips, still uncertain.

"I . . ."

A flare of unease raced through him at her sudden bout of nerves. Was he rushing her? Was she not yet prepared to surrender herself to the passions he could feel trembling through her body?

Adam gritted his teeth to try and control the desire raging through him.

He had sworn he would wait until the moment was right. Until she freely gave herself to him.

Even if it killed him.

And at the moment that seemed a distinct possibility.

"What is it, Addy?" he forced himself to ask in calm tones.

There was a moment's pause before she drew in a steadying breath.

"I do not know what to do."

He gave a faint frown. "What do you mean?"

"I do not know how to please you."

Giddy relief nearly sent him to his knees.

She was not frightened or disgusted by his touch, he thought with a dizzy pleasure. Instead she was concerned for his own needs.

His hands moved to frame her lovely countenance, slightly trembling from the force of his emotions.

"Addy, it is very simple," he said huskily. "Tell me that you desire me."

"Yes," she whispered.

His head bent slowly downward. "And that you want my kisses."

"Yes."

He teased her lips with light, feathery kisses, using his tongue to softly outline her generous mouth.

"And my touch . . ." he murmured, his hands following the delicate line of her neck.

She shuddered beneath his soft caress.

"Yes."

Wondering if he could possibly make it upstairs to his chambers or rather to simply carry her to the nearby sofa, Adam trailed his fingers along the provocative line of her gown.

His entire body clenched with a searing heat.

The sofa.

Definitely the sofa.

"Addy, I must . . ."

His rasping words had barely left his mouth when the door to the salon was thrown open and a shrill female voice pierced the air.

"Surprise, surprise!"

Chapter Eleven

Addy felt as if she had been tossed headfirst into an icy pond.

One moment she had been melting beneath the extraordinary sensations Adam was stirring within her and the next she was pulling away to gaze in horror at the open door.

Her horror did not lessen at the sight of the beautiful woman with dark hair and flashing emerald eyes. Or the short, thin gentleman with silver hair and elegant attire that joined the woman.

It was bad enough to have her evening alone with Adam interrupted. To have it interrupted by her flamboyant, unpredictable parents was the height of ghastly luck.

Blinking in the hope that it was all some horrid nightmare, she at last concluded they were not about to disappear.

"Oh my God," she muttered. "Mother."

Oblivious to the realization that she had clearly interrupted a romantic interlude, or even heard Addy's less than enthusiastic greeting, Lady Morrow smiled in a smug fashion.

"Darling, Addy, did we surprise you?"

Painfully aware of the silent gentleman at her side, Addy grimaced.

"That is one way of putting it."

Lady Morrow gave a tinkling laugh. "I told your father when we decided to travel to London that it would be such a surprise for our sweet Addy, did I not, Morrow?"

"No doubt you did." Lord Morrow yawned with obvious boredom. "There had been an incessant stream of words pouring from your lips since we entered the carriage. Thankfully I long ago discovered to ignore your babbling."

Lady Morrow cast a glare toward her husband. "Really, Morrow."

Knowing how swiftly her parents' conversations could deteriorate into flaming rows, Addy was swift to intervene.

"Mother, what are you doing here?"

Thankfully distracted, the older woman returned her attention to her daughter.

"Well, it had been so terribly long since we have seen you, my dearest. Naturally we thought to wait until you issued an invitation, but when one never arrived I decided you must have completely forgotten your poor mother. I was determined to discover for myself that you were well and happy."

It would have been a touching speech if Addy hadn't known quite well her mother was lying. Although her parents had always been fond of their children they had never troubled themselves to ensure they were well and happy. To them a child out of sight was indeed out of mind.

No, whatever had brought them to London, it had nothing to do with concern for her.

"I have written several letters assuring you that all was well," she pointed out in dry tones.

Lady Morrow waved a slender hand. Although well past forty she remained a beautiful woman with a sultry expression and a figure that was the envy of women half her age. It was little wonder gentleman of every age scrambled to attract her attention.

"A letter is not the same as seeing you with my own eyes. Any mother would feel the same."

"Perhaps most mothers," Addy muttered before she could halt the words.

"Addy." Lady Morrow widened her eyes with a pretense of shock. "Surely you are delighted to have us for a visit?"

"Actually . . ." Addy began, only to be interrupted as Adam stepped smoothly forward.

"We are, of course, quite happy to have you as our guests."

"Thank you, Adam," the older woman gushed, shooting Addy a chastising glance. "I should not wish to feel we were unwelcome."

Addy winced at her mother's less than subtle dig. "Of course you are not unwelcome, Mother," she forced herself to say. "I am merely caught off guard by your sudden arrival."

Her father gave a short laugh. "A nice way of saying she is horrified," he teased. "I told you that we shouldn't just descend like so much baggage."

Lady Morrow gave a loud sniff. "Nonsense. We are family."

"The very worse sort of guests," Lord Morrow concluded, echoing Addy's own thoughts. "You can't close the door on them, eh Drake?"

Adam gave a slight nod of his head. "No, I suppose not. Addy, why do you not ring for Mrs. Hall?"

With great reluctance Addy moved to tug the velvet rope. At the same moment Lady Morrow began a detailed inspection of the salon, her sharp gaze lingering on the priceless paintings adorning the walls.

"My is this not lovely? I have always desired a London

townhouse.'' She abruptly paused before an oil landscape. ''Oh my, is this an original?''

''Yes,'' Adam assured her. ''My father was a great collector.''

The older woman moved toward the bay window. ''And such a lovely view. I understand that there is a duke in the neighborhood.''

Adam's lips twitched with inner amusement and Addy breathed a faint sigh of relief. At least he wasn't furious at her parents' rude intrusion.

At least not yet, she reminded herself.

It was too much to hope that Lord and Lady Morrow would not create a whirlwind of chaos with them.

''We keep a stray one about to inflate our consequence,'' Adam said in suspiciously bland tones. ''He is, unfortunately, quite elderly and his heir apparent detests London. Soon we shall be reduced to an earl and two viscounts.''

Missing the humor in his words Lady Morrow heaved a sigh. ''How vexing.''

''Yes, indeed.''

Suddenly brightening, Lady Morrow turned back to regard the large room.

''Still, it is a well-situated house. You no doubt are besieged with visitors.''

A flare of alarm raced through Addy.

The mere thought of her mother's notion of entertainment was enough to make her swoon.

Memories of drunken poets, belligerent radicals, and gentlemen attired in nothing more than fig leaves flared through her mind.

Dear heavens, Adam would toss the lot of them into the street.

And she would not blame him.

''Actually we live very quietly, Mother,'' she said sternly.

''Quietly?'' Lady Morrow appeared genuinely baffled.

"Why on earth would you wish to live quietly when you could have all of London dancing attendance upon you?"

"I do not desire to have all of London in my home."

"Absurd." Her mother gave a click of her tongue. "If I owned such a setting I would be the most celebrated hostess in London."

Addy shuddered at the thought, but it was her father who took Lady Morrow to task.

"But you do not own such a setting, my dear. And Addy is mistress here. If she wishes to live quietly, then it is her choice."

A decidedly worrisome glint entered the emerald eyes. "She is no doubt merely intimidated. The ton can be so very fickle. With my guidance I am certain she shall soon discover just how simple it is to become the talk of the town."

Talk of the town?

Dear heavens, could anything be worse, Addy wondered.

"Mother . . ."

Addy's plea was interrupted as the housekeeper stepped into the room and regarded the unexpected guests in surprise. Adam once again took command of the situation.

"Ah, Mrs. Hall, would you please show Lord and Lady Morrow to the yellow chamber?"

"Certainly, sir." The servant glanced toward the older couple. "If you would follow me?"

Moving toward the door Lady Morrow blew Addy an airy kiss. "We shall see you in the morning, dearest."

Her father in contrast flashed her a wry grin. "Chin up, Addy. I shall endeavor to keep your mother from driving us all batty."

The sound of Lady Morrow chastising her husband could be heard as the trio moved down the hall and up the stairs to their rooms.

At long last, blessed silence returned to the room and moving to the sofa Addy collapsed onto the cushions.

Never in her wildest imaginings had she thought her parents would travel to London. At least not without a proper invitation.

Which was ridiculous, she sternly lectured herself.

When had her parents ever considered what was proper?

Although they would never deliberately cause another pain, they were like children who readily indulged their every whim. They never considered whether their actions might be inconvenient or even embarrassing to another. And they certainly never considered the notion that they should control their impulses. If it brought them enjoyment that was all that mattered.

Good heavens, what was she to do?

Visions of digging a deep hole in the garden rose to mind.

Her pleasant notion was brought to an end as Adam settled his large frame beside her and smiled in a rueful fashion.

"Well, that is a rather effective means of putting an end to an evening of romance."

Addy's expression was one of distress. "I am sorry."

He gave a shake of his head as he gently gathered her hands in his own.

"There will be other evenings, my dear." He smiled with wicked anticipation. "Or at least I hope so."

Although Addy appreciated his attempt to lighten her mood, her heart felt too heavy to respond.

The poor man obviously had no notion of the destruction her parents could wreak upon their quiet household.

If he did he would no doubt be fleeing in terror.

"No, I meant that I am sorry that my parents have descended upon us in such a fashion," she said in low tones.

He squeezed her hands in reassurance. "It is no doubt our own fault for not having invited them sooner. Frankly it never occurred to me that they might be concerned for your welfare.''

Addy gave an unladylike snort. "No doubt because they have never been concerned for my welfare before.''

"They did travel a goodly distance to see you.''

"Me? Fah.'' She turned to meet his steady gaze. She had already deduced the reason for her mother's visit. "My mother has always longed for a London townhouse. She has no doubt been counting the days until she could reasonably establish her claim upon your home.''

"Our home,'' he corrected in firm tones.

His gentle reminder only increased her misery. Adam had taken such an effort to please her over the past week. Never before had she felt so close to him. Never had her heart leaped and her breath quickened when he entered the room. Never before had she anxiously risen, eager to be out of her chambers and fly down the stairs to share breakfast with her husband.

Her marriage had suddenly seemed real. Her feelings for Adam had . . . well, to be perfectly honest, she had determined not to examine the odd tangle of warmth and breathless anticipation that assaulted her when she thought of her husband.

It was safer to simply enjoy the newfound peace.

And now that peace was about to be snatched away.

It was utterly unfair.

"This is terrible,'' she moaned.

"Addy.'' Reaching out he tilted her chin upward. The gray eyes closely inspected her drawn features. "What is it?''

There was little point in attempting to conceal her coiled fear. She did not doubt it was visible to the most obtuse soul. And no one could accuse Adam Drake of being obtuse.

"I may love my parents dearly, but we both know they will have this household in utter ruin before luncheon.''

Adam grimaced at the unarguable truth in her words.

"I can not pretend to be overly pleased by our visitors. Indeed, their timing could not be worse. But we can hardly throw them out of the house."

"You will be ready enough to throw them out when the salon is overrun with every radical, poet, and artist in London," she warned. "And, of course, there will be my mother's inevitable string of admirers."

He gave a dramatic shudder. "Gads, I do hope she does not decide to paint them in the nude. I do not believe poor Humbly could bear the shock."

Addy regarded her husband with a vague wariness. "Adam, surely you do not find this amusing?"

His fingers moved to lightly stroke her cheek.

"Would you prefer that I storm about the room in fury?" he asked. "It would change nothing."

She sighed. "No, I suppose not."

"Do not fret. We will somehow manage to survive."

"We might. I am not certain your reputation will."

"Allow me to worry about my reputation," he retorted.

"But you have always said . . ."

He pressed a silencing finger to her lips, a hint of regret upon his countenance.

"I think we have already agreed I said far too much in the early days of our marriage."

She felt a faint shiver at the intimacy of his touch. "You had some provocation, I fear."

His soft laugh brushed her cheek. "Surely we are not now to argue over whether I was a fool or not?"

It took a long moment before a shaky smile at last curved her lips.

"No."

"Good. I would much rather kiss you than argue with you."

That swirling heat attacked her stomach as his gaze slowly lowered to her parted lips.

When she had first learned of the prospect of her evening alone with Adam she had told herself it was the perfect opportunity to prove that she could change as well.

She would welcome his kisses, she had told herself. She would prove she was no longer a petulant child, but a woman who could bring him pleasure.

And from the moment he had entered the salon, she realized that it would take no effort to respond to his touch. For days he had teased her with his fleeting caresses. He had stirred to life a strange excitement that had haunted her days and made her restlessly toss in her bed at night.

She had been as anxious as Adam to celebrate their evening alone.

Now she felt a deep pang of frustration.

Blast her parents.

"You would rather kiss me?" she encouraged softly.

The smoldering glow returned to the gray eyes. "Most definitely."

"Oh," she murmured, her lips parting as he lightly nuzzled the corner of her mouth.

"Now, this is how I intended to spend our evening."

She arched toward him. "I see."

Adam gave a wicked chuckle. "I would rather you just feel."

Her hand raised to touch his lean cheek at the same moment the familiar voice of Vicar Humbly boomed through the room.

"Dear heavens, am I intruding?"

A dark cloud hung over Addy's head.

It had been three days since her parents had landed themselves in her salon and while the townhouse had not actually crumbled at their arrival, she knew it was only a matter of time.

Each day had been fraught with strain as her father plunged himself into the giddy pleasures that London had to offer and her mother grew increasingly restless in the placid peace that dominated the household.

Adam had wisely returned to his routine of devoting his time to the War Department, while Addy waited in dread for the scandal to explode.

And there would be a scandal, she had no doubt, glancing in annoyance at her mother, who leaned over her shoulder and made disapproving noises beneath her breath.

Addy had fled to her studio with Mr. Humbly in an effort to distract her nervous tension. She had hoped that an hour or two of working upon the portrait would help to ease her mind. But they had barely begun when her mother had burst into the room and promptly proclaimed the portrait was thoroughly unsatisfactory.

"Perhaps just an angel in the corner," Lady Morrow suggested in helpful tones.

"No, Mother."

"Well, at least add some color in the background. It looks positively dreary."

Addy gripped her brush so tightly it was a miracle that it did not snap.

"It is dignified."

"Nonsense. It is merely drab."

"Mother." Addy glared at the older woman in obvious warning.

"Oh, very well," her mother retorted peevishly. "It is your portrait. If Mr. Humbly does not mind, who am I to complain?" She abruptly straightened. "I believe I shall go and see if I can not discover a bit of excitement to liven this dull household."

Addy experienced a familiar sick sensation in the pit of her stomach.

Her mother in search of excitement was always dangerous.

"Not too much excitement, Mother," she warned.

Lady Morrow heaved a sigh. "Really, my dearest, you have become quite tedious since your marriage."

"No, Mother, this has nothing to do with my marriage," Addy corrected with a flare of insight. Since her marriage she had tried to paint her past with a rosy hue. Her resentment toward Adam had clearly befuddled her mind. It was only over the past few weeks that she had begun to realize that her life in the Morrow household had been anything but perfect. "I have never particularly enjoyed being embroiled in scandal. I just had no say in the matter when I was young. I do, however, have a say in this household."

Her mother gave a startled blink at her words. "Whatever do you mean?"

Addy narrowed her gaze. "No drunken poets, no opera dancers, no radicals that still smell of Newgate, and no naked gentlemen in my salon."

"Surely I am not to be confined to stuffy matrons?" Lady Morrow demanded.

Unrepentant, Addy gave a shrug. "You could always visit a museum or attend one of the numerous lectures being held throughout the city."

The older woman pressed a hand to the magnificent bosom, readily exposed by the crimson gown.

"Horrid. I would as soon return to Surrey."

Not willing to be manipulated by the shrewd woman, Addy offered a calm smile.

"Shall I call for your carriage?"

There was a tense silence before Lady Morrow tilted back her head to laugh with tinkling amusement.

"Very well. Ancient, creaking matrons it is. Until later, my dear."

With a casual wave of her hand, Lady Morrow swept from the room, leaving behind a far from comforted Addy.

She believed her mother would be satisfied with consorting with proper matrons when she sprouted wings and a halo.

Whatever her promises, Lady Morrow would do precisely what she desired, regardless of Addy's pleas. It was not that she deliberately desired to embarrass her daughter. She just could not help herself.

Slowly closing her eyes, Addy shook her head.

"Lord, give me patience."

"Did you say something, Addy?" Mr. Humbly inquired from his position across the room.

Forcing her eyes open, Addy grimaced in resignation.

"Merely requesting a bit of heavenly assistance."

The Vicar sent her a sympathetic smile. "Is it that bad?"

"My parents are not renown for their modest behavior or proper manners."

"No." His gaze became speculative. "But they will, indeed, add a bit of excitement to your household."

Addy gave a violent shudder. "That is precisely what I am afraid of."

Chapter Twelve

Addy knew she was being a coward.

As mistress of the house it was her duty to be with her guests. She should be ensuring their comfort, providing them with entertainment, and arranging visits to the various sights of London.

Instead she had ordered her breakfast to be served in her chambers and lingered long after she had attired herself in an apricot muslin gown and loosely arranged her curls atop her head.

It had been over a week since her parents had arrived and frankly she was weary of the daily battles with her mother. It was worse than having a spoiled child beneath her roof. There had been an endless stream of complaints of the boredom of Addy's life and at times loud tantrums when Addy refused to give a lavish ball. Her mother had sworn that she would expire from boredom if she were forced to spend one more day in the townhouse.

And as for Lord Morrow ... well, Addy chose not to

think about where her father disappeared to day after day. It was disturbing to contemplate the notion he was enjoying the delights of the local brothels or perhaps tossing away a fortune at the game tables.

At the moment it was easier to ignore his daily absences.

Staring out the window at the garden below, Addy heaved a faint sigh.

Would her parents ever leave?

For that matter, was Humbly ever to return to Surrey?

Would she ever be alone with her husband again?

A smile of pure irony curved her lips.

It was not that long ago she had thought she would give anything to avoid Adam. She would have welcomed Humbly, her parents, and perhaps the devil himself to act as a barrier between her and her husband.

Now she wished that they would all disappear and return her house to the peaceful, predictable establishment it had once been.

She wanted her evenings devoted to Adam, not pacifying her mother and apologizing to poor Mr. Humbly.

A sharp knock on her door forced Addy away from the window and across her chamber. She reluctantly suppressed the desire to ignore the summons, realizing she could not hide forever. Eventually she would have to make her way downstairs to face the predictable complaints and reproaches.

Expecting her mother, Addy was caught off guard as she opened the door to discover a young maid standing in the hall.

"Oh, Mrs. Drake, you must come immediately," the young servant cried the moment Addy came into view.

Addy's astonishment swiftly altered to sharp apprehension at the sight of the maid's harried expression.

Nothing good ever came from such an expression.

"Good heavens, what now?" she demanded, very much longing to slam the door in the girl's face.

"I . . . in the front parlor. Please, you must hurry," the maid stammered, offering a hasty curtsy before rushing back down the hall.

"Can there be no peace?" Addy muttered, forcing herself to leave the blessed comfort of her room. God alone knew what she would discover, she seethed as she marched down the steps. A menagerie gone mad, a lovesick fool threatening to plunge a dagger into his heart, or a belligerent buck hoping to put a bullet into her father.

The sound of raised voices could be heard long before she reached the salon and, tossing up a silent prayer for strength, she hurried forward and stepped into the room.

For a moment she could not comprehend what had caused such a panic. Her mother was calmly standing beside the chimneypiece, a tiny smile upon her lips. Otherwise, the room appeared empty. Then a series of grunts and gasps sent her gaze flying to the floor where two well-dressed gentlemen were determinedly attempting to choke one another.

She watched in horror as the gentleman beneath the other made a sudden surge to flip himself atop the other. The sudden action sent a delicate pier table wobbling and, rushing forward, Addy pulled it to safety as she glared at her mother.

"What the devil is going on here?"

Reluctantly pulling her attention from the combatants, Lady Morrow favored her with a brilliant smile.

"Ah, good morning, Addy."

Addy pointed furiously at the grappling men on the floor. "Who are these men?"

"Well, the one currently on the bottom is Mr. Dalmond and the one on top is Lord Powell."

Her mother's amusement only added fuel to Addy's temper.

"Why are they rolling about on my floor like a pair of idiots?"

Lady Morrow allowed herself a smug laugh. "I fear they are fighting over who will be allowed to pose as Hercules in my latest painting."

Addy threw up her hands in sheer disgust. "I said, no painting."

"Well you have forbidden me to entertain and your father has abandoned me to pursue his own pleasures," her mother retorted in defensive tones. "You can scarcely expect me to lay about this house doing nothing all day."

Addy's hands clenched in the need to grasp her mother and shake her silly.

"I expect you to keep your cicisbeos from brawling in my front salon."

The older woman glanced toward the grunting, red-faced gentlemen that appeared more akin to guttersnipes than pinks of the ton.

"I think it is rather charming."

"Mother." Addy gritted her teeth.

"What would you have me do?"

"Stop them."

Lady Morrow arched a superior brow. "My dear, no woman of sense attempts to come between gentlemen intent on doing one another injury."

"Damn." Realizing that she would have to take matters into her own hands, Addy stalked to the ridiculous nodcocks and kicked one of the legs that was sticking out. "Enough. Halt this foolishness at once."

Neither man paid her the least regard as they battled to gain the upper hand.

"Addy, I think perhaps . . ."

Her mother's words were cut off as a dark, ice edged voice sliced through the room.

"What is going on here?"

Addy breathed a sigh of relief as she turned to discover her husband striding rapidly toward her.

"Adam."

Barely acknowledging her presence Adam reached down to grasp the men by the scruffs of their necks. With tremendous strength he hauled the two of them upward and shockingly knocked their heads together. The men yelped in pain as with a disdainful expression Adam thrust them toward the door.

Both stumbled forward and angrily turned about to confront their assailant. It took only one glance, however, for them to blanch in fear as they discovered Adam regarding them with a frozen dislike.

"Out," he commanded, pointing toward the door. "Now."

"Yes, of course," babbled buffoon number one, backing his way to safety.

"Certainly. Pray forgive me," echoed buffoon number two, just as swift to make his retreat.

Within moments the house had regained its peace and Adam turned to regard his mother-in-law with a glittering gaze.

"I suppose this is your doing?"

Lady Morrow paled beneath his cold restraint, but as always she refused to take responsibility for her behavior.

"You needn't use that tone with me, Adam Drake. I have done nothing."

"You invited those fools here, Mother," Addy retorted stiffly.

"I could hardly be expected to know that they would become so violent."

"Something must have provoked them."

Lady Morrow gave an airy wave of her hand. "Who can say with young, hot blooded gentlemen? They are always so anxious to prove their manhood."

Addy gave a disgusted shake of her head. "I would say that all they proved is their stupidity."

"I found it all rather entertaining," Lady Morrow stubbornly argued, not seeming to comprehend the absurdity of having two grown men rolling about the floor like grubby schoolboys.

"No more guests," Adam abruptly cut into their squabbling, his voice sending a shiver down Addy's spine. He was no doubt furious at coming home to such a spectacle. And who could blame him? Any gentleman would be horrified. Especially a gentleman who possessed a spotless reputation.

"But . . ." her mother sputtered in outrage.

"You have heard Adam, Mother," Addy rushed to head off a dramatic scene.

A petulant pout marred the older woman's countenance. "I had no notion that our visit to London would be such a bore."

"Since you claimed that you came to ensure I am well, I do not comprehend how you could be disappointed," Addy pointed out.

The logic of her words made her mother scramble to regain her footing. She could not very well admit that she had merely used her daughter as a convenient means of settling in London. Not after her touching words of devotion on the evening of her arrival.

"Well, I did not realize that I would be a virtual prisoner in my own daughter's home," she at last grumbled.

"I regret that you are opposed to my rules, Lady Morrow," Adam said without the least hint of regret. "But I will not allow Addy to be distressed by your presence."

Addy shot her husband a startled glance. He was concerned for her? A sudden glow of warmth filled her.

Far less impressed with Adam's concern, Lady Morrow

gave a loud sniff. Adam stepped forward in an obvious threat.

"You will content yourself with enjoying your daughter's companionship or you will return to Surrey."

The older woman widened her eyes. "Really."

Adam opened his mouth as if to wrench a promise from his uncooperative mother-in-law only to be halted as a footman charged into the room.

"Excuse me, sir," said the young servant, awkwardly bowing.

Adam turned about to regard the intruder. "Yes?"

"I fear there has been a message from your club."

"My club?"

"Yes, sir." The footman swallowed a lump in his throat. "I . . . Lord Morrow has made something of a scene and the management is requesting that you come and collect him."

"Good God," Adam muttered.

Addy pressed a hand to her heart, desperately wishing that she could close her eyes and disappear.

"Oh, no."

"I shall leave immediately," Adam announced in firm tones.

"Very good." The servant was obviously relieved to have discharged his unpleasant duty and scrambled from the room.

Heaving a faint sigh, Adam turned and lightly brushed his lips over Addy's troubled brow.

"I hope to be home before dinner," he murmured.

"Adam . . . I am sorry," Addy said in broken tones.

He smiled ruefully. "You have nothing to apologize for, my dear. It is your father who shall be in my debt."

Lightly tapping her nose, Adam marched firmly from the room. Addy's heart felt as if it were made of lead. How could she have brought this terrible trouble upon his head?

By this evening all of London would be twittering over

the ridiculous scene in the salon and her father's outlandish behavior at the club.

She and Adam would be laughingstocks all over town.

A shudder raced through her as she thought of her husband's deep dislike for the tiniest hint of scandal.

Gads, he would be humiliated.

"At least I did not make a public spectacle of myself," said her mother, suddenly breaking the silence, her voice peevish.

Opening her eyes, Addy stabbed Lady Morrow with a killing glare.

"Oh, do be quiet, Mother."

Several hours later, Addy paced her studio in growing agitation.

Although her father had long ago returned to the house there had been no sign of Adam. His mysterious disappearance had preyed upon Addy with a gnawing fear.

What if he decided that he could not bear to be in the house?

Would he leave for their country estate without even informing her?

Or would he instead prevail upon a friend to allow him to stay with them?

Or worse, would he perhaps turn to Mrs. Wilton for the comfort she was so ready to offer?

Her imaginings grew progressively darker and more nonsensical as the minutes slowly turned into hours.

By late afternoon, she had herself convinced that even now Adam was closeted with his lawyer discussing the swiftest means of procuring a divorce.

What more final means of ridding himself of her and her madcap family?

It was something of a relief when the door to her studio

was tentatively pressed open and the dumpling form of Mr. Humbly entered the room.

"Hiding, my dear?" he asked with a small smile.

Addy heaved a harsh sigh. "I wish that I could. Unfortunately there was no large hole for me to climb into."

"Is it truly that bad?"

Addy wrapped her arms about her waist, battling back tears of self-pity.

"It is worse than you can imagine. This morning my mother managed to incite two coxcombs into a ridiculous brawl in the front salon and my father created such a scene at Adam's club that he was thrown out."

Humbly gave a sympathetic click of his tongue. "Oh dear."

"Poor Adam," Addy mourned. "He is probably wishing every Morrow to the netherworld, me included."

"Never that, Addy."

"How could he not?" Addy struggled to keep her voice steady. "My parents have been nothing but an embarrassment since they arrived."

Moving forward Mr. Humbly reached out to lightly pat her upon her arm.

"It is their way. They see nothing wrong with their behavior."

Addy closed her eyes, attempting to will away the burning sense of injustice. It was true that her parents had not done anything that they would not willingly have done within the confines of their own home. Or even that they had deliberately set out to cause a divorce between their daughter and Adam.

They had simply behaved precisely as they behaved every other day.

"I suppose," she grudgingly conceded.

"And, my dear, it was not that long ago that you wished

your household to be more like your childhood home," he reminded her gently.

"I must have been mad," Addy concluded with a shiver.

"No, merely human."

Uncertain what he was implying, Addy glanced at him in puzzlement.

"What did you say?"

Grasping her hand Humbly moved her to the nearby sofa and tugged her onto a cushion. Once assured she was settled he lowered his own bulk beside her.

"Do you know when I was a child we were rather poor?" he inquired with a rather searching gaze. "In truth, we were in straitened circumstances quite often."

Addy's confusion only deepened.

She hadn't the least notion what his childhood stories had to do with her current troubles.

"I am sorry."

Humbly gave a swift smile. "Oh, it did not bother me a great deal, although it did mean that I was often mercilessly teased by the local children."

Addy felt her heart tugged despite her distraction. It was unthinkable that anyone would be unkind to this gentle man.

"Children can often be cruel," she said softly.

"Yes, I can still recall their taunts when I attempted to join them on their rides with my poor, swaybacked pony. Hamlet was far too fat and lazy to keep up with the other horses and it only took them a few moments to be off without me."

Addy frowned in sympathy. "I suppose it must have made you very sad."

"Actually it made me angry and I found myself beginning to hate poor Hamlet. I blamed him for my unhappiness and begged my father for a mount that would allow me to race with the others."

Addy found herself regarding the Vicar with a faint sense

of suspicion. Did he have a specific point he was trying to make? It would be just like him to disguise a mild lecture in a seemingly reminiscent story of his childhood pony.

"Did he buy you one?" she asked slowly.

"No." Humbly gave a sigh. "My father wisely told me that when you have been given an animal to love you do not toss it aside like rubbish when you have tired of it."

"He must have been a good man."

"I did not think so at the time," the Vicar confessed with a sheepish expression. "I kept badgering him for a new horse until the local Earl overheard my complaints and sent a beautiful black stallion to me. I was delighted."

Addy lifted her brows at the obviously happy ending to his story.

"Ah, so you were allowed to race with the other children."

Surprisingly Humbly gave a firm shake of his head. "No."

"Why ever not?"

"Thunder proved to be a very high-spirited animal with a nasty habit of throwing me to the ground whenever I climbed onto his back and biting anyone foolish enough to stray near."

Much to her amazement Addy discovered herself biting back a chuckle at his woeful expression. It was very difficult to remain blue-deviled in the man's company.

"Oh no."

"Within a week my father had returned the monster to the Earl."

Addy reached out to lightly touch his hand.

"So you went back to poor Hamlet?"

The sherry eyes grew distant as he recalled his tumultuous days of childhood.

"Unfortunately I could not. My father had already given Hamlet to a family who desperately needed a horse to help with their farm work."

Addy smiled with sympathy. "So you had no horse at all."

Shifting on the cushion Mr. Humbly faced her fully. "No. I did, however, learn a valuable lesson."

Addy suddenly realized that Humbly did indeed have a purpose to his story. One that was no doubt meant to ease her turmoil.

"And what was that?"

"That it is quite natural to take what you possess for granted. Even at times to become bored with your blessings. Only the wise person takes the time to appreciate what he has been given."

Addy smiled wryly.

He was right, of course.

He was always right.

She had taken what she possessed with Adam for granted. Rather than appreciating his quiet dignity and the manner whereby he had always offered her a sense of security, she had only dwelt upon her sense of injustice.

Not that Adam should have written that absurd list of the behavior expected of his wife or made her to feel as if she could not be trusted to make the simplest decision for herself, a tiny voice reminded her.

Still, he had not been the ogre that Addy had built in her mind. And if nothing else he had offered her a measure of protection that had been sadly lacking in her parents' household.

And lately he had been offering far more.

A taste of Paradise.

If only her parents hadn't ruined it all.

She grimaced as she met Humbly's gaze. "Such as a peaceful household?" she said dryly.

"Precisely."

Addy heaved a regretful sigh. "I did not think I would ever say this, but I do wish I could have back those uncomplicated days. At the moment my nerves can not bear the strain.''

"You shall soon have even better days," Humbly promised with a smile.

Addy could only envy his confidence. She was not nearly so certain of her future.

"Perhaps."

"And you will have a greater appreciation of what you possess."

"Absolutely."

The sound of a distant gong brought an end to their conversation. With the eagerness of a gentleman who genuinely treasured the culinary arts, Humbly surged to his feet.

"Ah, dinner," he announced with relish, regarding her still-seated form with faint surprise. "Are you not coming?"

Addy would love nothing more than to remain in her studio and avoid her parents for the remainder of the evening. Unfortunately her duties as a hostess disallowed such temptation.

"I suppose I have no choice. I can not leave you to face my parents alone," she conceded, reluctantly pushing herself to her feet.

Humbly drew her arm through his own with a consoling smile. "They will soon be gone."

She gave a resigned shake of her head. Her husband had been driven from his own home. Her stomach felt as if it had been tied in a hundred knots. And her staff was beginning to regard her with pitying glances.

She rolled her eyes heavenward. "Not soon enough for me."

Chapter Thirteen

The townhouse was blessedly silent as Adam quietly made his way to his chambers.

A far cry from the chaos he had left earlier in the day, he thought with a heavy sigh. He had hated to leave Addy on her own to deal with the volatile Lady Morrow, but he had little choice, with Lord Morrow causing his own share of bedlam at his club.

It had taken nearly an hour to sober his father-in-law enough to lead him from the club and place him in the carriage. The ridiculous fool had locked himself in the cloak-room and refused to come out, claiming that the management had insulted him by refusing him more brandy.

Adam had barely shoved the sodden Lord Morrow into his carriage when he had been assailed by Lord Hoffman, who had claimed that the War Department had erupted into a pitched battle over the latest dispatches. Adam had seriously debated telling Hoffman to go to the devil. He had quite enough on his plate with his troublesome in-laws. And of course, poor Addy was nearly exhausted from worry.

He was clearly needed at home.

Unfortunately he could not completely turn his back on his duties to the government.

He had sworn a promise to do all that was possible for the soldiers overseas when he had become a war consultant, a promise that carried with it the burden of being responsible for the life and death of hundreds. He could not simply shrug aside that responsibility just because it was not convenient.

Finally, he sent Morrow home in his carriage and allowed Lord Hoffman to hurry him to the office. Once there, it had taken several hours of painstaking diplomacy to soothe the ruffled feathers and to seek a compromise that would satisfy the various parties.

All in all it had been a wretched day, he decided, entering his chamber and waving his valet out of the room. He wanted nothing more than to crawl beneath the covers of his bed and forget all about Addy's daft parents and the feuding politicians.

Pouring himself a glass of brandy, he slowly undressed and pulled on a heavy brocade robe. With an effort he forced his stiff muscles to relax. He would never sleep with his nerves coiled in tight knots.

He was just polishing off the last of his brandy when a soft knock on the connecting door made him turn in surprise.

"Come in," he called, waiting as his wife slipped into the room and closed the door behind her. Once again she was attired in that maddeningly provocative robe, but his attention was captured by the anxious expression that marred her delicate features. He instinctively moved to stand before her. "Addy, is something wrong?"

She gave a jerky shake of her head. "No, I merely wished to speak with you."

Adam breathed a faint sigh of relief. After the day he had endured he was uncertain if he could bear another disaster.

"You should not be up so late." He reached out to stroke her cheek with a teasing smile. "You will begin to have shadows beneath your eyes from your late evenings."

Her expression remained set in lines of strain as she searched his countenance.

"Where have you been?"

With a flash of insight Adam realized that Addy had been concerned by his long absence. He silently cursed the befuddled Lord Morrow. He had specifically requested the man to tell Addy he had been called to the War Department. Clearly such a simple task was beyond the fool.

"I fear that I was caught at my club by Lord Hoffman who insisted that I was desperately needed by Liverpool. An argument had erupted over the movement of our flanking troops."

There was a faint pause before he heard her soft sigh.

"Oh."

"I am sorry if you were concerned."

"I thought . . ."

Her voice broke off and his hand moved to cup her chin and press it upward. There was clearly something troubling her.

"What?" he demanded in tones that warned he would not tolerate being fobbed off. "What did you think, Addy?"

She gave a small shiver before she struggled to summon a weak smile.

"That you had perhaps fled London."

Adam could not hide his jolt of shock at her absurd words. "Why would I flee London? Has something occurred?"

"You know what has occurred," she retorted, her brows furrowed. "Those ridiculous men in the salon and then my father causing a scene at your club."

"It has been a difficult day," he agreed wryly.

"Yes."

He studied the wounded shadows in her eyes, his heart clenching with anger at her impervious, irresponsible parents.

"Far more difficult for you than for me," he said in gentle tones.

His words seemed to catch her off guard and she gave a shake of her head.

"How can you say that? It is your reputation that will be in shreds."

Adam had deliberately forbidden any thoughts of the obvious consequences of his in-laws' outrageous behavior. There was little use brooding on what could not be changed. Besides, he was far more concerned with his wife's growing distress.

"Perhaps a bit tattered about the edges but not in shreds, I trust," he assured her. "You, on the other hand, look as if you might shatter into a dozen pieces any moment."

She swallowed heavily. "I have been very worried."

Adam gave a click of his tongue, realizing that the dastardly Morrows were not entirely to blame for Addy's highly strung nerves. His own rigid lectures of propriety and respectability had clearly added an additional burden.

He silently cursed his priggish arrogance. Gads, he should have been smacked in the head.

"Addy, you cannot allow yourself to become so agitated," he urged firmly. "It has taken me days to ease that strain from your countenance. I do not wish it to return."

"But there is no telling what my parents might do next," she burst out, not willing to be easily consoled.

"Do not concern yourself with your parents. I will ensure they do not trouble you again."

Amazingly she appeared far from reassured by his promise. Instead she gave a sad shake of her head.

"Not even you can control my parents, Adam. They cannot help but create scandal. It is simply their nature."

That was true enough, he reluctantly conceded. Lord and Lady Morrow sought excitement the way a drunkard sought the bottle. No amount of threats or pleas would halt their foolishness.

It was obvious that he would have to take drastic measures to put an end to their bothersome presence in Addy's life.

"Trust me, Addy, I will handle the situation."

Something in his voice must have alerted her to his grim determination and the faintest hint of a smile touched her face.

"I feared that you would be furious."

Adam briefly recalled the unflattering words he had muttered beneath his breath as he had attempted to extract his father-in-law from the cloakroom.

"I am furious with Lord and Lady Morrow," he replied in all honesty. "But not with you, Addy. You have done nothing but try to halt your parents' antics. A task I do not envy."

Her features twisted in a revealing grimace. "No one would."

"True enough." He chuckled, his fingers moving of their own will to smooth the worried line between her brow. "Now enough of those frowns. I wish to see a smile upon those lips."

She studied him with a searching gaze. "You are not going to seek a lawyer and have this marriage put to an end?"

Adam felt a stab of surprise at her soft words. Dear heavens, surely she was not that uncertain of him? He would cut off his arm before he would allow her out of his life!

Clearly she needed to be reassured to the depth of his feeling for her. He gently framed her face with his hands.

"On the contrary, Addy. I am convinced that this marriage is just beginning."

"Just beginning?"

"We have spent far too much time at cross purposes," he said, recalling the barren early days of their marriage. "Neither of us was willing to forego our pride long enough to admit that we would be better served to work together."

He was thankful that a faint hint of amusement banished the lingering shadows.

"You do possess a lion's share of pride."

Adam arched a dark brow. "You have no small amount yourself, my dear."

"Me?"

"Yes." Before he could restrain himself Adam lowered his head to snatch a brief, blood-stirring kiss. "You."

With a faint sigh she arched toward him, her soft curves setting off all sorts of fireworks within him.

"Nonsense," she breathed.

Adam stiffened as lilac temptation curled about him. Blast. His control had been severely strained over the past few weeks and he no longer trusted himself to be able to restrain his hungry body.

He needed her so badly he trembled with the effort not to sweep her into his arms and override any lingering doubts.

"Addy," he at last croaked.

"Yes?"

"It is very late."

"So you have said," she retorted, not seeming to take his hint.

"Do you not think you should return to your chamber?"

Shockingly she pressed herself even closer to his stirring body.

"Do you wish me to return to my chamber?"

His teeth were clenched so tightly they hurt. "You know what I wish."

"No, actually I do not." Her hands slowly rose to stroke down the lapels of his robe. Adam's heart nearly halted as he thought of those hands against his bare chest. "What do you wish?"

His gaze burned a path over her upturned countenance. "To have you in my arms."

Her hands moved until her arms were boldly encircling his neck.

"Like this?"

"Addy." His arms convulsively encircled her waist, his blood rushing at a dangerous pace. "Do you know what you are doing?"

Her head moved forward to place a kiss upon the skin revealed by the opening of his robe.

"Pleasing you?" she whispered.

Adam nearly dropped to his knees at the fierce pleasure that exploded deep within him.

"Gads, yes," he moaned.

Her head tilted back as she offered him a seductive smile. "What else do you wish?"

The dam burst as white-hot desire poured through him. He could wait no longer and with a swift motion he had swept her off her feet and headed for the large canopy bed.

He had given her every opportunity to flee.

Now she was about to discover the true meaning of being his wife.

Addy awoke with a warm glow of good will.

For long moments she lay with her eyes closed as she tentatively probed the deep sense of happiness that filled her.

It was odd.

Yesterday had been a disaster.

First, her mother's ridiculous admirers battling in the

salon, and then her father making a drunken scene among Adam's friends.

She had spent the day in a tangle of dread and humiliation. She had been certain that Adam would be furious with her, so she had paced her room until his return. Then she had heard him preparing for bed and gathering her shaky courage she had forced herself to confront him.

She had gone to his chamber and . . .

The sudden memories of what had occurred next made her heart jump and a blush rise to her cheeks.

She knew without a doubt what it was that had left her feeling as content as a cat with a saucer of cream.

It had been a night of wonder.

A night of magic.

Suddenly nothing seemed to matter. Not her parents and their ridiculous behavior, or her suspicions that Adam might desire a more experienced lady. Not even the vague sense of fear that she had surrendered herself so completely to her husband.

She was utterly happy for the first time in her life.

With a decidedly gloating smile, Addy pushed herself to a seated position and gazed at the pillow next to her. Although the bed was disappointingly empty, she could still see the imprint of where Adam had laid his head and smell the scent of his sandalwood soap.

Running her hand over the indent in the pillow, her thoughts were distracted as the door was pushed open to reveal Adam carrying a large tray.

He looked impossibly handsome attired in a deep blue coat and black breeches. Her heart tripped as he gave her a lazy smile and crossed to the bed.

"Good morning, my dear."

Expecting to feel at least a measure of embarrassment for her eager response to Adam's caresses, Addy was rather startled to find she experienced nothing more than a warm glow as he sat on the bed and placed the tray across her legs.

"Breakfast in bed," she murmured, glancing at the numerous plates upon the tray. "It seems rather decadent."

He moved until she could feel the heat of his body through the thin sheet and offered her a wicked smile.

"I could have thought of far more decadent means of awakening you this morning."

A delicious thrill shot through her. "Adam."

He chuckled as he reached out to begin filling a plate with the vast array of food.

"What do you desire? Strawberries? Eggs? Ham?"

"Yes."

He arched a brow. "Yes, which?"

"Yes, all of them."

"What a glutton you are this morning."

"I am hungry," she retorted.

The silver eyes turned to a devilish smoke. "I wonder why?"

That tingle of anticipation returned at the obvious invitation in his expression, but even as she considered sweeping the tray out of their way Addy was struck by a sudden, unwelcome thought.

"Oh."

"What is it?"

"I completely forgot my parents." She heaved a rueful sigh. "They must be expecting us downstairs."

Pressing the plate into her hands, Adam regarded her with a hint of wariness.

"Actually, they are not."

"You have spoken with them?" she demanded in surprise.

"Yes."

His guarded manner warned her that he was attempting to hide something from her.

"What has occurred?" she demanded.

He paused before giving a resigned shrug. "I had hoped we could enjoy breakfast before we spoke of your parents."

Addy steeled herself for the worst. When it came to her parents, absolutely anything was possible.

"Tell me."

"I requested that they pack their bags and leave," he said in clipped tones.

Expecting to hear news of some new disaster, Addy gave a blink of surprise.

"What?"

Clearly misinterpreting her confusion for anger he heaved a heavy sigh.

"I am sorry, Addy. I realize that it was high-handed of me to toss your parents out of the house without even discussing the matter with you, but frankly I could not bear another day."

"I do not blame you, Adam," she hastened to reassure him. "It is a wonder that you endured them as long as you did."

"I did not ask them to leave for me. I did it for you."

She searched the features that had become so dear to her. "Why?"

His expression abruptly hardened at her soft question. "Even the most senseless gentleman could realize that they were making you miserable."

Addy slowly smiled. It was still an astonishing sensation to realize that anyone would care for her happiness. It would take time to accustom herself to the knowledge.

"They are trying on one's nerves," she agreed.

His hand clenched on the sheet. "I can bear a few brawls in my salon and even rescuing my father-in-law from my club, but I will not allow you to worry yourself to death."

A dangerous tenderness clutched at her heart as she regarded his set expression, a tenderness that was precariously close to love.

Swiftly Addy attempted to distract her willful thoughts.

"How did they take your announcement?"

As she had hoped, his expression lightened and a hint of amusement entered the silver eyes.

"Your mother screeched that she would not be parted from her beloved daughter while your father muttered something rather uncomplimentary about stiff-rumped bores."

Addy shuddered even as she gave a sudden chuckle. She had no doubt her parents had given a masterful performance. No one could outdo the Morrows when it came to tragic scenes.

"I am sorry."

"I am not." He startled her by saying in satisfied tones, "It gave me the opportunity to inform them that I consider their treatment of you selfish and utterly unacceptable. They are not to return until they are capable of treating you with the respect that you deserve."

She regarded him in admiration. His courage was clearly remarkable.

"Dear heavens, my mother must have been swooning."

"She did attempt a brief faint, but when I left her upon the floor she gamely rose to her feet so she could continue her lecture on the evils of leaving her daughter alone in the clutches of such a coldhearted blackguard," he said dryly.

"I almost wish I had been there to witness the scene."

He shook his head at her teasing words. "No, you were far safer here. Your mother launched half a dozen figurines across the room when she realized I was not about to relent. It was sheer luck no one was injured."

Addy's heart froze in dismay. "Oh no, not the Dresden!"

"No, they were a few of the ones we received from Aunt Clara. No great loss."

She breathed a faint sigh of relief. She would not put it past her mother to destroy a priceless collection in a fit of pique.

"Thank God."

With an air of determination Adam reached for a strawberry from her plate and pressed it to her mouth. Instinctively Addy bit into the ripe fruit and savored the sweet tartness.

"Let us forget your parents," he urged, reaching for another strawberry. "We shall instead concentrate on how we intend to spend our day."

Allowing him to feed her, Addy gave a faint shrug. She was too lazily content to trouble herself with thoughts of the day ahead.

"What do you wish to do?"

Without warning Adam waggled his brows in a wicked motion. "Surely you know better than to ask me what I wish?"

"Really, Adam" she protested, even as her heart somersaulted with excitement. He had suddenly become incorrigible and she discovered she did not mind a whit.

He laughed as he reached for a napkin to wipe his fingers.

"Actually, I thought we might take a stroll."

Addy couldn't halt her surprised glance toward the window. Even from this distance she could see the sky was overcast and a heavy drizzle was falling.

"But it is raining."

He slowly smiled. "I have a mind to see you barefoot in the rain once again. Unless the proper Mrs. Drake is too stuffy for such a delightful pastime?"

Her eyes glittered at the subtle challenge and she set aside the tray as a reckless pleasure raced through her.

"Mrs. Drake will never be too stuffy," she assured him with a bold smile.

Leaning forward he claimed a heart-stealing kiss.

"Thank God," he whispered against her lips.

Chapter Fourteen

The ball gown had been delivered earlier that day.

Pulling the delicate concoction from the tissue, Addy had been initially delighted by the shimmering bronze satin embroidered with pearls. Cut off the shoulder it possessed tiny puff sleeves and a dark bronze ribbon encircled the high waist.

It was not until her maid had actually slipped the gown over her curves that she realized just how revealing the neckline had been cut. Even worse, the sparkling diamond necklace that Adam had given to her drew immediate attention to the vast amount of white skin exposed.

Leaning forward Addy anxiously studied her reflection in the mirror. There was nothing precisely indecent about the gown, she tried to assure herself. Most, if not all the ladies would be wearing similar attire. Many with necklines far lower than her own. It was only that her curves were rather generous that made her feel so exposed.

That and the fact she had become accustomed to gowns

that would have suited the most prudish governess, she reminded herself.

Absently arranging a raven curl that had been artfully arranged to brush her temple, Addy drew in a deep breath and slowly turned to face her waiting maid.

"Oh, Mrs. Drake, you look beautiful," the girl obligingly cried as she pressed her hands together.

Addy self-consciously raised her hands to the neckline. "You do not believe it is cut too low?"

The maid gave a shake of her head. "Not half so low as most ladies will wear."

"Still . . ."

"It is lovely," the servant firmly insisted, her hands placed on her hips as if prepared to physically restrain Addy from choosing a more modest gown.

Addy smiled ruefully. "I do hope that Adam agrees."

"You hope that Adam agrees to what, my dear?" A dark voice drawled from the connecting door.

With a jolt of surprise Addy turned to watch her husband stroll toward her. Her breath was sucked from her lungs at the magnificent sight of him in formal attire. The stark black was a perfect foil for his powerful form and elegant features. Even the gray eyes appeared to glitter with a brilliant silver sheen.

Dark, dangerous, and utterly thrilling.

And all hers, she thought with smug triumph.

Intent on one another neither noticed as the maid dropped a hasty curtsy and moved toward the door. Nor did they catch sight of the girl's cheeky grin as she escaped from the nearly tangible electricity in the air.

"Good evening, Adam," Addy murmured, vibrantly aware of the manner in which his gaze narrowed as it swept over her elegant form.

"Another new gown?"

Although his tone was mild, Addy discovered herself

stiffening in a defensive manner. For some reason it was important that he not condemn her choice out of hand.

They may have come a vast distance over the past weeks, but there was still a vulnerable part of her that needed to know he truly trusted her. That he could allow her to be herself and not some shallow image of his perfect wife.

"Yes."

His gaze lingered upon the plunging neckline. "It is very ... delectable."

"You do not approve?" she demanded in flat tones.

Perhaps sensing her tension, Adam abruptly lifted his gaze and offered her a wry smile.

"Addy, if I had my way you would be muffled from head to toe each time you left this house. It is a gentleman's tendency to desire to keep his wife's loveliness to himself."

Her chin jutted upward to a stubborn angle. She had endured a stomach full of proper gowns, she told herself, conveniently forgetting her own doubts upon the decency of the gown.

"I will not go to the ball muffled from head to toe."

He gave a slow shake of his head. "No, you shall wear your new gown and no doubt be the most beautiful woman in the room. I do, however, reserve the right to bloody the nose of any gentleman I catch ogling you."

Her tension eased at the faint hint of teasing in his tone. She had feared a stern lecture that would have stolen all pleasure from the evening.

Lowering her lashes she glanced through them in a flirtatious manner.

"Why, Mr. Drake, you sound almost jealous."

The gray eyes flared with ready desire as he stepped close enough for her to be wrapped in his heat.

"Insanely and unashamedly jealous, Mrs. Drake," he confessed without hesitation.

A heady pleasure shivered through her at his possessive

gaze. "Very well, you are free to bloody the nose of any gentleman who ogles me," she graciously conceded, her smile provocative. "As long as I am free to return the favor for any female who sinks her talons into you."

He chuckled as he reached out to encircle her waist with his arms.

"Why, Mrs. Drake, you sound almost jealous."

Just a few weeks ago Addy would have sliced out her tongue before admitting such a weakness. She had been far too resentful, and perhaps even too frightened, to reveal any vulnerability to her husband. Now, however, she tilted back her head to regard him with open honesty.

"Insanely and unashamedly."

He drew her closer with a low growl of satisfaction. "Do you know what I think?"

"What?"

His head lowered to stroke his lips over her cheek and down the line of her throat.

"That it would be far more pleasant to remain quietly at home rather than being battered and bruised at a stuffy ball."

Addy was rapidly coming to the same conclusion as familiar swirls of excitement danced through her stomach. Adam had only to touch her to make her melt with pleasure and this occasion was no different.

What woman with the least amount of sanity wouldn't prefer to remain in her chambers with a handsome, skilled lover rather than be squashed by a crowd of chattering strangers?

Unfortunately her building desire could not entirely dismiss her realization that it was a poor hostess who constantly disappeared with her husband when a guest was patiently awaiting her arrival downstairs.

She and Adam had abandoned the poor Vicar far too often during the past week.

"We can not forget Mr. Humbly," she forced herself to

mutter as the lips nuzzled the sensitive line of her collarbone. "He will be leaving at the end of the week."

For a moment the lips continued seducing away her good intentions. Then, just when Addy had decided the Vicar could fend for himself, Adam heaved a regretful sigh and pulled away.

"I thought that I was the one boringly chained to duty and responsibility?" he mourned.

She gave a wry smile as she smoothed the crushed fabric of her gown.

"I fear Mr. Humbly has been a reprehensible influence upon you. Over the past few weeks you have become a veritable rogue."

"While you have become positively proper," he teased, reaching up to trail a finger along the deep curve of her neckline. "At least upon most occasions."

She playfully knocked his hand away with her fan. "We must go down. Mr. Humbly will be waiting."

"Oh, very well," he reluctantly conceded, holding out his arm.

Together they left the chamber and walked down to the front salon. The house was blessedly silent without the provoking presence of Lord and Lady Morrow, and while Addy occasionally felt a faint pang of remorse at the knowledge they must be furious at having been tossed out the door, she did not regret Adam's decision for even a moment.

It was sheer delight to awaken in the morning without the burning fear she was about to face disaster. Or even to work upon her portrait without her mother's unceasing complaints.

Of course, she could not entirely regret her parents' tumultuous visit, she reminded herself. Mr. Humbly had warned her to appreciate what she possessed. After her parents' chaotic presence she fully appreciated the silent peace of her household.

Stepping into the room, Addy smiled as the Vicar hurriedly rose to his feet.

"My dear, what a lovely gown," he said with an admiring gaze.

"Thank you, Mr. Humbly. Might I say you are looking very dashing yourself?"

The Vicar dropped his gaze to his own dark coat and pantaloons with a sorrowful sigh.

"Very kind of you, Addy, but I fear I never appear dashing. I can never seem to keep all my bits and pieces together."

Addy could not help but laugh at his complaint. It was true his coat was already rumpled and his cravat askew, but his sweet smile and amiable disposition more than compensated for any lack of elegance.

"I think you look charming," she insisted.

The Vicar turned to smile at Adam. "Perhaps we should leave before your wife quite turns my head."

Addy stifled a yawn as she glanced about the sea of guests that had currently pushed her and Mr. Humbly into a distant corner.

Although she had tried to muster a bit of enthusiasm for the Vicar's sake, she discovered the minutes dragging past with painful slowness.

Even with her new gown she had no desire to twirl about the dance floor or to encourage the numerous male gazes that strayed in her direction.

In truth, she wanted nothing more than to return home and be alone with her husband.

Addy gave a faint shake of her head. Who would ever have suspected that she would one day desire a dull, uneventful evening with Adam?

It was hardly the stuff of schoolgirl dreams. But at the

moment she could think of nothing more delightful than being cuddled upon Adam's lap in front of a warm fireplace.

Glancing toward her companion, Addy grimaced at the round countenance flushed with heat and the manner in which the Vicar occasionally winced at the shrill giggles as desperate debutantes attempted to be noticed among the crowd.

Poor Mr. Humbly.

He looked nearly as miserable as herself.

"It is very crowded," she said, hoping to ease his discomfort.

He leaned forward, clearly unable to hear her above the loud din.

"I beg your pardon?"

"It is very crowded," she shouted over the noise.

"Indeed," he agreed, then his eyes widened. "Oh dear."

"What is it?"

"A matron in a turban. Mind your toes, my dear."

He pulled her deeper into the corner as a large countess stomped past missing Addy's toes by a mere breath.

"Good heavens." She rolled her eyes heavenward. Enough was enough. Not even her toes were safe in this crush. It was time to retreat. "I believe I shall find Adam and see if he is prepared to leave."

There was no mistaking the sheer relief that rippled over the Vicar's countenance.

"A fine notion, my dear."

She reached out to pat his hand in sympathy. "Wait for us in the foyer. I will not be long."

Sucking in a deep breath, Addy plunged her way into the crush, grimacing at the overpowering perfumes and the numerous male hands that reached out as she passed by.

Gads, she would be black and blue before she ever discovered Adam, she thought with a stab of impatience.

Only sheer perseverance allowed her at last to battle her

way to the far door and, drawing in a deep breath, she scanned the dance floor for a sign of Adam.

Not seeing his familiar form she had turned her attention to the numerous gentlemen huddled beside an open French door when a hand suddenly clamped her elbow with surprising force.

Abruptly turning her head, Addy discovered Lord Barclay regarding her with a glittering gaze.

"Addy, at last," he drawled with his most charming smile. "I have struggled to reach your side all evening. Unfortunately you have been surrounded by the most persistent admirers."

Stifling her instinctive impatience with the shallow dandy, Addy forced a polite smile to her lips.

"Lord Barclay."

"I do hope that you have saved me a dance?"

"Actually I was just searching for Adam so we can take our leave."

He arched a golden brow. "Surely not so early?"

"Yes."

The too-handsome features seemed to harden at her obvious indifference to his determined pursuit. No doubt he expected every female to swoon with appreciation at his manly charms, she thought with an unusual flare of cynicism.

"I begin to think that you are avoiding me."

She bit back the urge to inform him that she would be delighted never to encounter him again. His constant flirtations were becoming wearisome.

"Nonsense," she politely denied. "I am simply fatigued by the crush."

His lips twisted with a hint of mockery. "And anxious to be home with your husband?"

She met his gaze squarely. "Very much."

There was a stiff silence before his expression cleared and he offered a half bow.

"Of course. I believe I saw him headed toward the card room. Allow me to escort you."

Although disliking the thought of remaining in the company of the notorious rake, Addy had little choice but to accept his offer.

"If you wish."

Steering her through the nearby door Lord Barclay halted as they came upon a vast crowd just leaving the supper room.

"We shall never make our way through," Barclay announced, abruptly tugging Addy across the hall and thrusting her through an open doorway. "We shall find a less crowded route."

"Where are we going?" Addy demanded as he gave her a firm shove forward and she noted they had entered a deserted library.

"Why, to find the flawless Mr. Drake, where else?" he retorted with a return to his earlier mockery.

"I do not think . . ." Addy's words stumbled to a halt as she turned about to discover Lord Barclay firmly closing the door and then turning the key in the lock. "What are you doing?"

"Just ensuring a bit of privacy," he retorted, turning about to face her as he slipped the key into his pocket.

"Privacy?" Her brows snapped together. "Why should we have need of privacy?"

He gave an ugly laugh. "Not even you are that naive, my dear Addy."

Her bewilderment swiftly hardened to anger as she regarded him with distaste. If this was some sort of joke it was not at all amusing.

"You will call me, Mrs. Drake, my lord," she informed him in icy tones. "And I demand that you unlock that door immediately."

Her captor strolled forward. "I think not."

"What?"

"I have waited far too long to have you alone. You have been annoyingly elusive."

Addy backed to the center of the room, more annoyed than alarmed.

"Are you foxed?"

"Merely drunk upon my desire for you," Barclay retorted, continuing his path toward her.

"If you are not foxed then you must be mad. I demand that you release me at once."

Halting before her, the nobleman regarded her with a taunting smile.

"You are in no position to demand anything, Mrs. Drake."

"I shall scream."

"No, you will not," he said in confident tones. "Just think of the scandal you will cause if you are discovered alone in the room with me. And we both know how desperately your paragon of a husband dislikes the faintest hint of scandal."

He was right, damn him, she seethed. She would never bring such scandal upon Adam. Not that she was about to admit as much to this wastrel.

"I shall tell them you forced me into this room," she warned.

He shrugged. "And I shall say that you lured me here and then lost your nerve when it came to the sticking point. It will be a toss-up to discover whom the ton will believe. In either event there will be a deafening thunder of gossip for weeks to come."

Her hand itched to slap his handsome face. Only the knowledge such an action was bound to make the situation worse restrained her.

"Why are you doing this?"

His gaze deliberately swept over her neckline. "I said you were naive."

"Balderdash," she snapped.

Barclay gave a sharp laugh. "What a poor opinion you possess of your charms. You husband is clearly not performing his duties."

"You are not so desperate for a woman that you need force one against her will."

"Thank you, my dear."

Her nose flared with distaste. "What do you want?"

He paused for a moment before folding his arms across his chest. "If you must know the truth, my dear, my first desire was to annoy Adam."

"Why?"

A sudden sneer twisted his lips. "You cannot imagine how extraordinarily tedious it was to be forever in the shadow of Adam Drake. At school he was the darling of every teacher. The rest of us were constantly berated for not living up to Drake's scholarly excellence. He even managed to thrash us upon the sporting field. And of course, he never created the least amount of trouble. He was utterly perfect."

Addy did not bother to hide her pride in her husband. "Adam can hardly be blamed for being superior to you at school."

"Oh, it was not just at school that I was forced to be lectured upon the numerous attributes of your husband," he continued, the hard glitter in his eyes sending a faint trickle of fear down her spine. "My own father was forever throwing Adam's sterling character into my face. Adam never gambled or drank his evenings away. Adam did not toss his allowance away on opera dancers. Instead he nobly sacrificed his life to the efforts of the War Department. It would be enough to make any gentleman sick to his stomach."

"Sick with jealousy, you mean," she said before she could halt the words.

He lifted an indifferent shoulder, the firelight dancing over his countenance and adding a hint of menace to his too-perfect features.

"Perhaps. In any event, I decided that it might be a great deal of fun to bring the high and mighty Drake down to the level of the rest of us mortals. And what better means of destroying a gentleman's arrogance than by seducing his wife?"

Addy's stomach turned at his sordid plot. What sort of man deliberately seduced a woman for petty revenge?

"A pity for you that I have no desire to be seduced."

"Actually it is a pity for you," he said in low, mocking tones.

A rash of unease prickled over her skin. Although she tried to assure herself this man would not harm her with a hundred guests just outside the door, she could not wholly deny there was something unnerving about the dark anger that smoldered in his eyes.

Jealousy.

Envy.

And the bitter resentment of a weak man toward a stronger, more powerful will.

A dangerous combination.

"What do you mean?" she demanded in a steady tone, thank heaven.

Without warning he reached out to grasp her chin in a cruel grip.

"Had you simply given in to my advances, we could have enjoyed a delightful few weeks before I allowed Adam to discover our relationship. As it is, you shall be punished as a straying wife without any of the enjoyment."

"You are mad." She twisted away from his grasp to glare at him. "Adam will never believe I betrayed him."

Barclay laughed easily at her fierce words. "You know very little of a gentleman's pride if you think he will not suspect the worst. Especially a man such as Adam. Why, he nearly called me out for merely speaking with you.''

His words struck her with the force of a blow.

How would Adam react if he found her alone with a handsome rake?

Their relationship had altered over the past few weeks. They were closer, bound tighter and far more intimate than ever.

But she could not forget the memory of his anger when he had found Barclay with her at the ball.

How furious would he be to discover she had been locked alone with Barclay for goodness knew how long?

Her heart clenched in fear.

No, she could not bear to lose him.

Not now.

Not when she had just fallen in love with him.

Realizing that Barclay was watching her with a smug amusement, Addy abruptly squared her shoulders.

She would not allow this horrid wretch to suspect that she doubted Adam's trust for a moment.

Maybe, just maybe she could escape before any true damage was done.

"Perhaps you are so fickle, my lord, but not Adam," she forced herself to retort.

"Fah." He waved a dismissive hand, utterly confident in his power to have his revenge. "He may have ice in his veins, but even Adam will be male enough to suspect the worst when he discovers you in my arms.''

She shuddered with sheer loathing. "It is little wonder your father found you such a disappointment. You are a pathetic creature.''

Fury rippled over his countenance as he reached to grasp her upper arms.

"And you are in need of a lesson in manners, my sharp-tongued shrew.''

"Let me go."

"Not a chance."

With frightening ease he hauled her closely against his body. At the same moment, the muted sound of Adam's voice floated through the air.

"Addy. Addy are you in there?"

"Adam," she cried, struggling to free herself. "Please, help me!"

Chapter Fifteen

With a strength he did not even know he possessed, Adam slammed into the locked door and crashed it open.

Thank God he had seen Barclay hauling Addy into the room from his position down the hall, he told himself, stumbling into the library. Although it had taken an eternity to battle his way through the crowd, he held on to the hope that there would have been no time for the lecher to harm his wife.

Shoving the broken door shut to avoid the passing guests who had, thank God, been too involved with a brawl in the card room to note his odd actions, Adam turned to face the couple in the center of the room.

Heady relief flared through him as he realized Addy appeared tousled but safe. His relief only deepened as she angrily stomped on Barclay's toes before rushing to Adam's side.

His relief swiftly sharpened to fiery fury, however, as his gaze swept over the nonchalant nobleman.

"Barclay," he said as if it were a curse.

The rake calmly smoothed his golden hair. "Really, Drake, do you have no sense of decorum at all? I think it should be perfectly obvious that Addy and I desired a bit of privacy."

Adam never allowed his burning gaze to waver. "Addy, please find Humbly and wait for me in the carriage."

"Adam, you must listen to me," she said in urgent tones.

Adam gritted his teeth. His control was hanging by a thread. He did not want his wife to witness the violent outburst that was about to explode.

"Not now, Addy."

"But it is not what you think."

He growled deep in his throat, "Just go."

"He forced . . ."

"Addy, we will discuss this later," he snapped, turning to flash her an impatient frown. As much as he might desire to pull her into his arms and comfort her, he knew that his emotions were too raw. He wanted her out of the room so that he could murder Lord Barclay without her watching in horror.

She simply stared at him for a taut moment then, with an expression of sharp disappointment, she gave a nod of her head.

"Very well."

He reached out to halt her as she turned and made her way to the door. He forced his hand to drop, however, as he realized he could not reassure her now.

Lord Barclay had harbored an irrational dislike of him since their days at Oxford. A dislike that had festered over the years. Obviously it was time that they cleared the air once and for all.

She may be disappointed by his purely male need to punish Lord Barclay for his treacherous behavior, but somehow he would make her understand that he had no choice.

Waiting for the door to close behind Addy, Adam slowly turned to meet Lord Barclay's mocking gaze.

"Rather abrupt with your dear wife, were you not, Drake?" he taunted, clearly unaware of the danger crackling in the air. Of course, the buffoon had never been overly blessed with intelligence, Adam reminded himself, his hands curling to tight fists. "It is little wonder that she was so anxious to seek a bit of solace with a gentleman who comprehends the needs of a woman."

Smiling with cold intent Adam stepped forward and smashed his fist into the sneering face. Barclay fell to the floor with a satisfying thump and raised a hand to his nose that was copiously bleeding.

"If you speak of my wife again, I will slice you open and shove your cowardly heart down your throat."

Dumbstruck by Adam's sudden attack, Barclay rose unsteadily to his feet and glared at his opponent.

"There is no need to bully me, Drake. I only came in here with Addy because she claimed you did not concern yourself with her peccadilloes. Had I . . ."

Adam's fist once again connected with the bloody nose, sending Barclay sprawling onto his back. This time he possessed the sense to stay down.

"I warned you not to speak of my wife."

"Bloody hell." Barclay scooted across the carpet, his mocking expression changed to one of wary pain. "I did nothing but accept a blatant lure. What would you have me do?"

Adam laughed with icy disdain. Perhaps a few weeks ago he would have been goaded by such words. He had been too uncertain of Addy, too fearful that he had ruined whatever chance of happiness they had by his sheer arrogance.

Now he merely found Barclay's words ridiculous.

Addy would never betray him.

He would stake his life upon it.

"You belong in Bedlam if you think for a moment I would believe Addy came in here willingly." He flicked a disgusted glance over the elegant form now rumpled and marred with a spattering of blood. "She would as soon bed a snake."

An ugly anger flared in the pale eyes. "What would you know of Addy's . . ." His words were abruptly cut off as Adam took a deliberate step forward. Cringing on the carpet, Barclay glared at him in impotent fury. "Dammit, Drake, you have already broken my nose."

"That is only the first of many things I intend to break," Adam warned.

Barclay's eyes narrowed with a cunning desperation. "I would be very careful unless you wish the entire ton to discover I was locked in this room with your wife."

Adam had expected no less from the spineless creature. He had always known Barclay was a weak-willed coward. Why wouldn't he be willing to destroy the reputation of an innocent woman to save his own hide?

"You breathe one word of scandal concerning Addy and I will personally geld you."

The man paled, but he gave a shake of his head. "Fah."

With a flick of his wrist Adam allowed the knife he kept hidden in his sleeve to drop into his hand. Only a fool traveled about London without some protection. And he had never been a fool.

"Shall I do it now?"

"You . . . you can not threaten a nobleman."

"I can do anything I wish." Holding up the wicked blade Adam smiled with a chilly determination. "Do not forget that I possess very powerful friends. They would be willing to turn a blind eye to any misbehavior as long as they have need of my services."

"My father will have something to say about that," Barclay attempted to bluster.

"Your father, like the rest of society, considers you as nothing more than an embarrassment," Adam retorted. "He would not risk the wrath of the Prince to save your sorry soul. He might even thank me for ensuring you are no longer capable of littering the town with your by-blows."

The stark truth of Adam's words made Barclay's features twist with fury.

"Damn you, Drake."

"What is it to be, Barclay? Your silence or your manhood?"

There was a moment's pause as the rake attempted to gather the necessary nerve to boldly damn Adam to do his worst. Then with an audible snap of his teeth he glared into Adam's unrelenting countenance.

"My silence," he choked out.

Adam narrowed his gaze. "One whisper and I will track you down, no matter where you flee. That is a promise."

"Go to hell."

Satisfied that he had properly intimidated the fool, Adam forced himself to perform a mocking bow. He had to leave before he gave in to his pounding need to beat the nobleman senseless.

"Always a delight, Barclay."

Adam was restlessly pacing the floor of his bedchamber when a muffled sound through the connecting door brought him to a halt.

He had deliberately avoided Addy since their return to the townhouse. His temper still simmered at a dangerous level and he had no wish to inadvertently hurt his wife's feelings by snapping at her like an injured dog.

Now, however, he discovered himself moving instinctively to open the door and step into her chamber. After the events of the evening she might be finding it difficult to fall asleep, he told himself with a pang of remorse. He should have considered her distress earlier.

Rounding the canopy bed he expected to find Addy pacing the floor, much as he had been doing. Instead, he discovered her jerkily moving from the wardrobe to the bed where she was stuffing her belongings in an open portmanteau.

A bolt of shocked disbelief flared through him.

"Addy, what the blazes are you doing?" he rasped.

She did not even glance up as she thrust a peach gown into the bag.

"Packing."

His brows snapped together with impatience. "I can see that much. Why are you packing?"

"I must leave."

He suddenly stilled with fear. "Has something occurred? Your parents . . ."

"My parents are fine," she broke in with sharp tones.

"Then what is it?"

"I cannot stay here. Not after tonight."

Adam felt as if he had been slapped.

Dear God.

He had sensed she was upset, but nothing had prepared him for this.

"Because of Barclay?" he demanded, hoping he could indeed lay the blame upon the lecherous scoundrel. It would give him another reason to smash his handsome countenance. "I assure you that he will never be troubling you again."

"No." She at last raised her head to reveal her pale countenance and blazing eyes. "This has nothing to do with Lord Barclay. It is you."

He clenched his teeth, feeling as if his stomach were being wrenched inside out.

"I apologize Addy, that you witnessed me losing control of myself in such a manner. But when I saw Barclay's hands upon you I wanted to murder him. I did not mean to frighten you.''

She blinked as if startled by his strained words. ''I was not frightened of you, for goodness' sake.''

''Then you were offended that I wished to punish, Barclay?'' he demanded in disbelief. ''Addy, not even a saint could have witnessed the brute manhandling his wife and not retaliated. And I have never claimed to be a saint.''

''Really, Adam, for such a clever man you can be incredibly dense,'' she snapped.

Adam threw his hands up in defeat. ''Obviously I am incapable of reading your mind, Addy, so why do you not just tell me why you must leave?''

Her lips trembled, but she forced herself to meet his gaze squarely.

''Because you still do not trust me.''

Adam regarded her with stunned amazement. ''What?''

''I saw your expression, Adam,'' she cried in low tones. ''You were furious.''

He reached out to grasp her shoulders, barely preventing himself from shaking some sense into her.

She had frightened him half to death.

''Good God, of course I was furious. I just told you that I nearly murdered a peer of the realm.''

She glared at him with barely concealed pain. ''You were also furious with me. You believed that I went with Lord Barclay willingly. You would not listen to a word I wished to say.''

''And that is why you must leave? Because you think that I do not trust you?''

He felt her tremble beneath his hands. ''I cannot forever be worried that something I might say or do will prove that I am unworthy of your faith. It is like living with a guillotine forever poised above my neck.''

Adam gave a shake of his head. It had never occurred to

him that she might fill her head with such nonsense. Not after they had grown so close.

"You are being absurd, Addy."

The dark eyes shimmered with unshed tears. "Am I? Can you say that you did not suspect that I had joined Lord Barclay in that room of my own will?"

"My dear, I may not be a polished rake, but even I can tell the difference between a woman enjoying a man's embrace and one who is fighting to be free," he said in dry tones. "To my knowledge no woman who desires to be seduced has ever stomped upon a gentleman's toes to encourage him."

A hint of uncertainty rippled over her pale features. "But you were so cold to me. You ordered me to leave as if I were some misbehaving child."

Belatedly Adam realized how his behavior had encouraged Addy to believe the worst.

He briefly closed his eyes as he heaved a regretful sigh.

"Forgive me, but I did not wish you to witness me becoming violent. I did not want to frighten you more than you already had been."

She carefully searched his countenance as if seeking the truth upon his features.

"And what of the carriage ride home? You could not even bear to glance in my direction."

His grip loosened so he could lightly stroke the stiff lines of her shoulders.

"I was still battling to regain my temper. Having been denied the satisfaction of throttling Barclay I was forced to ease my fury with mere thoughts of what I wished to do with his wretched hide."

"You do not think I wished to be with Lord Barclay?"

"Not for a moment." Adam gently cupped her face. His heart clenched at the vulnerability that shadowed the dark eyes. Gads, he had to convince her that he would never hurt her! "I do trust you, Addy. I trust you with my name, with my life, and with my heart. Now and forever."

He held his breath as a slow, tentative hope began to bloom deep in her eyes.

"Oh Adam, I was so afraid that we had lost what we had discovered," she whispered.

"Never, my dear," he declared in fervent tones. His hands trembled with the force of his emotions. "I love you. I love your wonderful spirit and kind heart and your passionate nature."

Her breath caught before a glorious, near blinding smile banished the last of her doubts.

"And my crazy relatives?"

Adam gave a sudden chuckle. "I love them because they somehow managed to create you. It is a miracle that I will never take for granted again."

Without warning she threw herself against him. "I love you too, Adam."

More than pleased to have a warm bundle of feminine curves pressed to his body, Adam obediently wrapped his arms about her waist.

"I cannot promise not to be stuffy and boring," he warned, burying his face in her satin hair.

"You are not stuffy or boring," she loyally denied. "You are an honorable gentleman who faces his responsibilities and can always be depended upon. That is precisely what I love most about you."

Adam's heart felt as if it might actually burst. Dear heavens, he had never thought he could be this happy.

Pulling back, Adam regarded her with a provocative smile. "Well, I do have a bit of wickedness in me. Would you desire me to offer you a taste of my dark secret?"

Her dark eyes glittered with the lure of a temptress. "I do prefer a proper gentleman, but I suppose I could be convinced to have a small taste of wickedness."

A gentleman who had been trained always to accommodate a lady's request, Adam instantly scooped her off her feet and headed for his chamber.

"Then allow me to convince you," he murmured.

Vicar Humbly was feeling decidedly smug.

Granted it had taken longer than he had initially predicted to bring Adam and Addy to their senses. And there had been a few uneasy moments when he had harbored a doubt as to his ultimate success. But in the end love had triumphed, as was only proper.

With a sense of contentment, Humbly glanced toward the couple standing arm and arm in the foyer. There was no missing the glow upon their faces or the secret glances they shared.

Yes indeed, he had done a fine job as Cupid, he preened as he reached down to pick up the small bag set beside the door. His work here was now complete and it was time to concentrate on poor Beatrice and her new husband.

"You are sure you must leave?" Addy demanded as he placed his new hat upon his head.

"Yes indeed, my dear. I have imposed upon you far longer than is proper."

"Nonsense," she denied with a lovely smile. "We have enjoyed having you with us, have we not, Adam?"

The gentleman offered his wife an indulgent glance before turning his attention to Humbly.

"Absolutely. You have made a most welcome change in this household."

Humbly gave a shake of his head. The situation seemed to call for a measure of modesty.

"Any change was not made by me, I assure you."

Adam's gaze was shrewdly knowing. "Nevertheless, we owe you a great deal."

"All I ask is that you remain as happy as you are at this moment," Humbly assured him.

Adam slipped an arm about his wife's shoulder, a deep contentment settling about them.

"That is a request that is easily granted."

Humbly did not doubt his assurance for a moment. Their love may have taken time to develop, but it would be more resilient and enduring for their trials.

"Now, I must be on my way," he said firmly. "I have a most pressing fear that Mrs. Stalwart is even now tossing my beloved books into the fire. Do not forget to have the portrait sent to the Vicarage, my dear."

"The moment it is finished," Addy assured him, moving forward to offer him a brief hug. "I shall miss you."

Deeply touched he reached up to pat her cheek. "As I shall miss you."

"Take care, Humbly," Adam said as he moved forward to join his wife.

"Of course."

Turning toward the door Humbly was suddenly halted as the housekeeper abruptly entered the foyer carrying a large basket.

"A moment, Mr. Humbly."

With more than a bit of curiosity he watched the woman move toward him.

"Yes, Mrs. Hall?"

"Here." She roughly shoved the basket into his hands.

"What is it?"

The woman regarded him in a stern manner. "One can never depend upon those horrid posting inns to provide a proper meal."

Humbly gave an appreciative sniff of the delectable aroma filling the air.

"Lemon tarts?"

"And some sliced ham, a loaf of bread, and a nice jug of fresh milk."

Humbly hid a smile. The housekeeper had barely tolerated his presence for the past few weeks. He could only wonder if her sudden display of friendship was made because of Adam and Addy's obvious happiness, or merely out of relief that she was about to be rid of him.

In either event he was promised a delicious meal before returning to Surrey and cucumber sandwiches.

"This is a very generous gift," he murmured.

Mrs. Hall appeared awkwardly self-conscious. "Well, we cannot have people thinking we begrudge our guest a proper meal."

"Thank you." Humbly offered his sweetest smile. "It will help to make the journey more tolerable."

"Just see that you eat every bite," the woman commanded before turning and surging her way back toward the kitchen.

"Well, it seems that you won over Mrs. Hall at last," Addy said in surprised tones.

Humbly grimaced. "Or perhaps this is her means of ensuring that I do not linger for a last meal," he said ruefully. "In any event I shall enjoy the feast. God bless you, my children."

Determined not to be distracted again, Humbly moved through door held open by the patient butler and down to the waiting carriage. Allowing the groom to help settle him upon the leather seat he pulled the basket onto his lap and opened the lid.

Sweet aroma filled the carriage, and, plucking out a delectable tart, he barely noticed when they began rattling down the cobbled street.

With a wide smile he bit into the pastry and allowed his eyes to close with sheer pleasure.

"Ah . . ."

ABOUT THE AUTHOR

Debbie Raleigh lives with her family in Missouri. She is currently working on her next Zebra Regency romance, A CONVENIENT MARRIAGE, which will be published in December 2002. Debbie loves to hear from readers and you may write to her c/o Zebra Books. Please include a self-addressed stamped envelope if you wish a response.

More Zebra Regency Romances

__A Taste for Love by Donna Bell $4.99US/$6.50CAN
    0-8217-6104-8

An Unlikely Father by Lynn Collum $4.99US/$6.99CAN
    0-8217-6418-7

__An Unexpected Husband by Jo Ann Ferguson $4.99US/$6.99CAN
    0-8217-6481-0

__Wedding Ghost by Cindy Holbrook $4.99US/$6.50CAN
    0-8217-6217-6

__Lady Diana's Darlings by Kate Huntington $4.99US/$6.99CAN
    0-8217-6655-4

__A London Flirtation by Valerie King $4.99US/$6.99CAN
    0-8217-6535-3

__Lord Langdon's Tutor by Laura Paquet $4.99US/$6.99CAN
    0-8217-6675-9

__Lord Mumford's Minx by Debbie Raleigh $4.99US/$6.99CAN
    0-8217-6673-2

__Lady Serena's Surrender by Jeanne Savery $4.99US/$6.99CAN
    0-8217-6607-4

__A Dangerous Dalliance by Regina Scott $4.99US/$6.99CAN
    0-8217-6609-0

__Lady May's Folly by Donna Simpson $4.99US/$6.99CAN
    0-8217-6805-0

Call toll free **1-888-345-BOOK** to order by phone or use this coupon to order by mail.

Name_____

Address_____

City_____ State_____ Zip_____

Please send me the books I have checked above.

I am enclosing $_____

Plus postage and handling* $_____

Sales tax (in New York and Tennessee only) $_____

Total amount enclosed $_____

*Add $2.50 for the first book and $.50 for each additional book.

Send check or money order (no cash or CODs) to:

Kensington Publishing Corp., 850 Third Avenue, New York, NY 10022

Prices and numbers subject to change without notice.

All orders subject to availability.

Check out our website at **www.kensingtonbooks.com.**